The Rose Queen

The Rose Queen

Justin Mitson

Contents

Dedication   1

1   CHAPTER ONE   3

2   CHAPTER TWO   13

3   CHAPTER THREE   19

4   CHAPTER FOUR   30

5   CHAPTER FIVE   35

6   CHAPTER SIX   47

7   CHAPTER SEVEN   59

8   CHAPTER EIGHT   66

9   CHAPTER NINE   74

10   CHAPTER TEN   80

11   CHAPTER ELEVEN   86

12   CHAPTER TWELVE   97

13   CHAPTER THIRTEEN   103

14   CHAPTER FOURTEEN   114

15   CHAPTER FIFTEEN   124

About the Author   134

Dedication

To my daughter, Aurora,

Watching you grow, achieve, battle back from obstacles, and rise to every challenge fills me with immeasurable pride. Keep forging your path with courage, wisdom, and grace—there is no limit to what you can accomplish.

With love,
Dad

Red Team Ink
DBA of Zealot Solutions, Idaho LLC
9480 River Beach Lane
Garden City, ID 83714
Copyright © 2025 by Red Team Ink

All rights reserved. Without limiting the rights under the copyright reserved above, no part of this publication may be reproduced, stored in, or introduced into a retrieval system, or transmitted in any form or by any means (electronic, mechanical, photocopying, recording, or otherwise) without prior written permission.

This is a work of fiction. Names, characters, businesses, places, events, and incidents are either the products of the author's imagination or used in a fictitious manner. Any resemblance to actual persons, living or dead, or actual events is purely coincidental.

For permission requests or information about discounts for special bulk purchases please contact: redteamink@gmail.com. Substantial discounts on bulk orders are available to corporations, professional associations, and small businesses.

Printed in The United States of America
ISBN 979-8-3485-5283-1
Title: The Rose Queen
Description: First Edition
Editing and cover design by Donna Lane

{ 1 }

CHAPTER ONE

Snowy closed her eyes and inhaled the sweet scent of the dark pink roses. The new rose bush that had cropped up in the yard was small, but it had a strong, intoxicating fragrance. It seemed like a perfect homecoming after some long, treacherous weeks away on the *Gillfish 2*. She hadn't realized how much she'd missed Epping until they'd landed at her cottage on the forest's edge.

"Snowy! Minty!" Claudette's daughters, Annelise and Camille shouted as they ran toward the *G2*. Snowy looked down and saw another little girl with them, with Claudette not far behind. She turned around and saw Goldie, sitting on Clem's shoulders. Then she noticed that Minty was staring at the girl with Claudette's daughters.

"That can't be," Minty said, barely above a whisper.

Snowy shook her head and looked again. The girl looked almost exactly like Goldie.

"Are we home?" Goldie squealed, running across the deck and jumping on Minty's back.

"Yes," Snowy said. "Home at last."

As Carter and the crew dropped the sail-bridges, Snowy eagerly disembarked.

"Welcome home," Claudette said, giving Snowy a hug. "But I must say, I didn't expect the ship to land in the yard."

"Neither did I," Snowy said. She looked back at Minty, who was holding onto Goldie with one hand and carrying the scepter of the trees in the other. "Just a minute ago, we were in the Bavarian Forest and then—"

She had rapid flashes of a red dragon, Bessie the yak, ogres, bloodhounds, squirrels, and an old book. Her leg throbbed briefly and she shook her head. Claudette's daughters and the other girl ran toward Minty and Goldie. "You know what? It doesn't matter. I'm just glad to be home."

"I'm glad, too," Claudette said. "I've kept up the cottages for you and Minty. And I hope you're hungry. I'll have a nice supper for you later."

Snowy watched the little girls playing in the yard, then turned toward the new rose bush. "Yes, famished," she said. "Claudette, I don't recognize that rose bush over there. Did you plant it?"

Claudette shook her head. "No," she said. "Although it's funny that you say that. I assumed it was here before I arrived, and maybe I never noticed it. But it just popped up one day."

"How odd," Snowy said. "How long ago was that?"

Claudette shrugged. "Maybe two weeks ago? I'm not sure. Like I said, I assumed I hadn't noticed it."

"Interesting," Snowy said, noticing that Carter and Clem had joined Minty, Goldie and the other girls in a spontaneous game of tag. "And, who's that girl with your daughters? Is she a friend of theirs?"

"Oh, that's Belle," Claudette said. "She also popped up one day."

Snowy jerked her head around. "Sorry, what?"

Claudette rubbed her hands on a dish towel tucked into her apron. "It was the strangest thing," she recalled. "We were inside your cottage late one evening. I was cleaning the kitchen, and the girls were working on their sewing. I looked out the window and saw this girl, walking out of the forest, all by herself. It was just before sundown and she looked lost. I opened the door and she walked in like she'd been here before. And she's been here ever since."

"Really? What do you know about her?"

"Not much," Claudette said. "She's not very talkative, but she doesn't seem to have any family. Given that you had helped all the orphans escape Mr. von Brock's factory, and that you've visited the orphanage on the other side of Epping Forest, I figured you wouldn't mind if she stayed here. At least for now."

"Oh, no, no," Snowy reassured. "That's fine. It's just so peculiar. Do you think she came from the orphanage?"

"I asked," Claudette said. "She said she didn't, but she couldn't tell me anything else. I sent word to the orphanage and the lady in charge, oh, I can't remember her name—"

"Mrs. Hayhurst," Snowy said.

"Yes," Claudette said with a nod, "her. She said she'd never heard of her, and that they hadn't had any new children in a while."

"And surely you've noticed that she looks just like—"

"Oh yes," Claudette said. "In fact, at first I thought it was her."

Snowy watched Belle playing with Goldie, awed by their resemblance to each other. "Very, very peculiar," she said. "Well, I think I'd like to freshen up. And I imagine we'll have the crew here, at least for the day. Do you suppose we have enough to feed everyone? If not, we have some supplies on board."

Claudette crossed her arms and smiled. "No one will go hungry on my watch," she announced. "I'll get right on it."

Snowy stepped into the cottage and took in the familiar scenery. Claudette had kept everything neat and tidy, with tiny bud vases of roses throughout the rooms. Galileo leaped down from his spot on the sofa and curled himself around her legs with a hearty purr. She knelt to pet him. "Hello, old friend," she said, stroking his forehead. "It's good to see you." With a flick of his tail, he untangled himself and went back to his nap in the fading sunshine. So, she went to her wash bowl and splashed fresh water on her face. Then she unbraided her hair and brushed it out. She went back to the front of the cottage and peered out the window.

Minty, Carter, Clem, and the girls were still playing on the grass as Claudette puttered about in the kitchen.

"Will your friends eat *choucroute garnie?*" she called.

"I don't even know what that is, but they'll eat anything," Snowy reassured. "I can't remember how long we've been at sea."

"It's an Alsatian dish," Claudette explained. "Sauerkraut with sausages and potatoes. I might throw in some bacon to make sure I can feed everyone."

"Sounds perfect," Snowy said, her eyes still focused on the front lawn as she tied her hair back. "Thank you, Claudette. You've done a great job looking after things while we were away."

Claudette shrugged again. "I'm so happy to be out of Bonn," she said, her eyes dampening. "You've given my girls and me a wonderful new life."

Snowy could see how sincere Claudette was. "I'm glad it worked out," she said. "I'm going back outside for a while. Please let us know if you need any help."

"Oh, Miss Snowy, I almost forgot," Claudette said, wiping her hands on her apron. "There's a letter for you on the table. It arrived from London about a week ago."

Next to a vase of roses, Snowy saw an envelope. She recognized the seal immediately. The Royal Observatory.

"Oh, it must be from John Flamsteed," she exclaimed. "How wonderful."

A puzzled look crossed Claudette's face.

"He's an astronomer," Snowy explained. "We met him before we went to Bonn. In fact, it was at the Royal Observatory that we first met Mr. von Brock."

Picking up a butter knife from the table, she carefully opened the envelope.

"Dear Miss Snowy and Miss Minty,

I trust that you have enjoyed a relaxing journey to the Caribbean—"

Snowy stopped reading long enough to let out a hearty laugh. Then she continued.

"Sir Christopher Wren, the Duke of Somerset, and I are eager to hear about your trip. In the meantime, I'm writing to tell you about some interesting events that have been transpiring in London.

"King Charles II is beginning to fall out of favor with the common people. While he has been incredibly supportive of our endeavors at the Royal Observatory here in Greenwich, I'm afraid he doesn't have much of a rapport with his subjects. The general consensus is that he has overburdened them with taxes and laws they feel are punitive toward those of lower economic stature.

"Furthermore, many of his subjects feel that their needs for safe, hygienic housing are not being met. Many of them work multiple jobs to keep their families fed and then come home to squalor. As you know, after the Great Plague a few years ago, people are highly concerned about disease. And they believe the monarchy isn't doing enough to keep its people safe.

"However, one bright spot has been the revitalization of the royal garden in Hyde Park. It's quite lovely and is abloom with many fragrant blossoms these days. King Charles built a wall around the garden after he returned from exile and it's off-limits to commoners. But one can easily view its splendor through the gates.

"I do hope you'll come and visit us soon at the Royal Observatory so that we may compare notes and share research, at your convenience, of course.

Sincerely,

John Flamsteed"

As Snowy finished the letter, Minty opened the cottage door.

"There you are," she said. "I was wondering where you went." Carter and the little girls piled into the cottage behind her.

"We got a letter from John Flamsteed," Snowy said, showing it to Minty. "He wants us to come to London."

"But we just got back," Minty said. "What are you going to tell him?"

"LONDON!" Goldie squealed. She clapped her hands together. "When do we leave?"

Claudette had a hard time concealing her giggle. Meanwhile, Belle sat down next to Galileo and scratched his chin.

"Hello," Snowy said, crouching down next to the girl. "My name is Snowy. And I hear your name is Belle."

The little girl nodded and kept petting Galileo.

"I understand you've been staying here," Snowy continued.

Again, the girl nodded without looking up. She had straight black hair and almond-shaped eyes, just like Goldie.

"Belle," Snowy said, "It's fine if you don't want to talk. But I want you to know you're welcome to stay here as long as you'd like."

Finally, the girl looked up, a smile brightening her face. "Thank you," she said in a whispery voice.

"When are we going to London?" Goldie asked, tugging on Snowy's skirt. "I want to see the big city!"

"Well," Snowy said, "I guess we should figure that out. I suppose we could sail in a few days."

"No," Carter said, "not yet. We damaged the rudder and keel when we landed here in Epping. We can work on it here, but it would be better to take it to the shipyard at Maldon."

"But how will we get it there if we can't sail?" Minty asked.

Snowy smiled. "I know a way."

***

Minty squinted as she walked from her cottage toward the *G2*, looking toward the rising sun. Carrying a small tray of coffee and blackberry muffins, she crossed the grass. Having a ship in the meadow between her house and Snowy's certainly wasn't the oddest thing she'd seen lately, but it still gave her pause.

"Good morning," a familiar voice called from the railing at the bow.

She looked up and smiled at Carter, the golden rays of the sunrise spreading out behind his handsome face like a halo as he pulled on his shirt.

"Good morning," she said, blushing and looking away as he dressed. "I, uh, I thought you might want some breakfast."

"For me? That's nice of you," he said as she approached the sail-bridge. "But wait, I'll come down there."

Minty felt her pulse surge as he hopped down from the side of the sail-bridge. Landing a few feet in front of her, he tumbled into a somersault, then popped up to his feet and took the tray from her hands.

"I'll carry that," he said with a bow.

Startled by Carter's acrobatics, she laughed. "You must be hungry."

"Starving. Let's sit over here," he said, nodding toward the shady spot near the dark pink rose bush at the forest's edge. When they got there, he set down the tray, then took her hand and helped her to a spot that would keep the sun out of her eyes. "This looks amazing. Did you make these?"

"Yes," Minty said, offering him a blackberry muffin. "I couldn't sleep so I started baking. I do that sometimes, when I get lonely and start thinking about—" She stopped, exhaling a heavy breath, and suddenly filled with sadness.

"Your family?" he asked, his hand on her cheek.

She choked back tears and nodded. "Yes," she finally said, laying her hand atop his. "I just get this way sometimes. I don't know why."

"Because it's sad to be alone," Carter offered, his eyes fixed on hers.

She could see gentleness and understanding in his gaze. Too often, she forgot that he'd lost his family, too, and instead focused on her own grief. As the weight of the moment descended on her shoulders, she looked away again.

He poured a cup of coffee and handed it to her. "Because it's normal to miss your family. There's nothing wrong with those feelings, Minty."

She composed herself and sipped her coffee. "I guess you're right," she said. "And I know you've been through it, too. How do you get past it, Noah?"

He filled the other cup and held it to his lips. "You don't," he said. "But at some point, you realize that you'll have your own family, and, hopefully, things will be better."

"Race you!" Goldie squealed as she ran past their picnic, with Belle, Annelise, and Camille chasing after her.

Minty and Carter both lunged for the coffee pot to keep it steady as the girls whizzed by. Its delicate china lid rattled, and it lurched to one side, but fortunately it stayed upright. As the girls giggled behind them, Minty and Carter caught their breath, then burst out laughing.

"That was close," Carter said, taking a bite out of muffin.

"Kids can be rambunctious," Minty replied.

"But they can also be a blessing," he said, wiping his mouth. "I mean, I know I want to have kids someday."

"Oh, so do I." She looked at him and imagined what kind of father he might be. Maybe the kind that held little girls' hands and endured their tea parties but still showed them how to tie a bowline or wield a sword, if the circumstances dictated such things to be necessary.

"I'm glad the coffee pot didn't break," he said, snapping her out of her thoughts.

"Me, too. My mother gave me that coffee service," Minty said.

"Ah," he said. "So, it's both special and pretty. Just like you."

Minty's green eyes stared in disbelief as she wondered if she'd heard him correctly. For a while now, she had felt an attraction to the good-looking Noah Carter with the mysterious middle name. But she hadn't been sure it was mutual. He was always chivalrous and polite toward her, but then what did she expect from a first mate?

And besides, they'd been busy sailing the Atlantic, taking on pirates, blowing up child labor factories, battling frog men and sea monsters, and settling feuds between squirrels. There hadn't been much spare time for romantic pursuits. But since they'd landed, literally, back in Epping, she'd felt a sense of permanence. As if she was ready to reinforce her roots and finally allow herself to be where she belonged. And she was sure that Noah was somehow part of that.

But it was no mistake. He leaned toward her, his face warmed by the sunrise. Her hands shook as he inhaled the heady scent of roses, thick in the morning dew, and fresh blackberries ushered him closer. Eyes locked, he put a hand in her auburn hair and laid a soft kiss on her forehead. Then he drew back, as if suddenly unsure.

"Sorry," he said. "I shouldn't have—"

Minty put her hand over his. "I don't mind," she said, her pulse and stomach now fluttering as she wished he'd do it again.

"No, I—"

"What are you two doing?" Annelise asked.

Minty spun around and saw that Annelise and Goldie were watching a butterfly that had landed on the rose bush while Belle and Camille looked for clovers. Realizing Annelise was talking to the other girls, Minty turned back to Carter, who was sipping his coffee as if he'd die of thirst without it.

"Noah," she started. "I know you have to take the *G2* to Maldon soon."

At last he put down his empty cup. "Yes, we'll have to repair the rudder and keel," he said. "Might be a few weeks. We'll have to see how bad it is and how long we have to wait for materials."

"I'm going to miss you while you're gone."

"I wish you could come with me," he said. "But I know you're going to London."

"Well, I'll be with you for a little while. I'll go with you to Maldon first. Snowy said that we can use the scepter that WC Squirrel gave us in the Bavarian Forest. As long as we have that, we can jump from place to place. All we need is another piece of wood and we can make it back. So, we'll get the ship to Maldon, and then she and I can come back here."

"Why not just jump to London from Maldon?"

"Because we'll need a carriage, and clothes, and a few other things," Minty said. "Besides, Goldie wants to go to London. And it'll be nice to get back to the big city, even if it's only for a short time. It's an exciting place with just as many adventures to be had as there are at sea. But I think she should stay here while we take the *G2* to Maldon. She hasn't really had a home. I want her to be able to stay with Claudette for a little while before we leave."

Carter nodded. "That sounds like a good idea."

The girls had run off to play with Clem and it was quiet again. Minty watched them climb on his back as if he were a pony and then she turned back to Carter.

"Noah, do you really want a family some day?"

He put his hand over hers, then pulled it to his lips and kissed it gently. "I do."

Minty blushed. "Well, maybe when you get back, we should talk about that."

"I'll look forward to it," he said, clasping her hand tightly now. "Just promise me something."

"What's that?"

He smiled wide as he squeezed her hand. Then he put a finger on her nose. "Don't go off to London and meet some fancy chap who promises you excitement and adventure."

{ 2 }

CHAPTER TWO

"Rosaleen! Rosaleen!"

The king was in another foul mood, apparently, stomping through the royal garden with no regard for the tiny succulents and manicured hedges that had been nurtured for months.

Rosaleen pushed her long black hair out of her eyes with the back of her grimy hand, smudging her chiseled cheekbone. The cameo around her neck bobbled as she swung around.

"Yes, your majesty," she called from behind a trellised wall laced with ivy as she watched him trample a row of begonias. "I'm over here."

She slipped her pruning shears into one of the many pockets in her olive-green work trousers and smoothed her matching shirt, which was beginning to dampen in the midday heat. A forced smile crossed her full lips as she dipped into as much of a curtsy as her muddy work boots would allow.

"Rosaleen, whatever have you done with the reflecting pool? I distinctly recall requesting white flowers, not blue," he huffed.

"You asked for delphiniums, your majesty," the soft lilt in her voice betraying her familiar frustration. "You said you'd seen them at the Palais-Royal in Paris, when your mother was, well, *visiting* there, and that you must have them. I asked which you preferred, and you told me blue. I sent for them from Paris and they just arrived a few weeks ago. I remember it clearly."

"No, I must have white," he huffed again like a child who'd had his toys taken away. "Don't you think I've heard the discord spreading like another plague among our communities, filling dark spaces through whispers and fermenting in hearsay? The public is losing its trust in the monarchy. They've begun to question my motives when it comes to raising taxes and I don't need to be trifled with that kind of troublesome speculation. I must present my subjects with a symbol of the purity of the British crown to keep them appeased. This simply will not do. Rip them out and plant something else. Immediately."

Rosaleen swallowed, trying to stave the anger bubbling up in her gut. "But it will take a long time to replace that many plants, and to get them to grow to a suitable height, like the blue delphiniums eventually did."

"That is not my concern, Miss Bramble. Perhaps you should've thought this through. And how dare you question me to begin with? I should have you fired."

She paused, again quelling her anger and letting his harsh tone hang in the humid air. Her fingers brushed over the handle of the pruning shears in her pocket, a subtle reminder that she was not unarmed. "My apologies," she said, her crooked smile exposing the slight gap in her front teeth. "I only want to be sure I understand what you want. What would you suggest, your majesty? You see, in that spot, with the full sun, there are only certain varieties—"

"Rosaleen, don't make me remind you that *you're* the expert, but you serve at *my* command," the king said, waving his hand dismissively. "I'm allowing you to keep your job, for now, because you've managed to turn this royal garden into a place where my wife enjoys spending time. And the more time she spends here, the less time she spends with *me*."

"Perhaps lily of the valley," Rosaleen offered.

"You figure it out."

"Yes, your majesty," she said, curtsying again as he turned and strode away.

When she was certain he was out of earshot, a heavy sigh escaped from her petite frame. Her emerald eyes turned to the reflecting pool at the end of the garden, beyond the boxwood hedges she'd been grooming into an elaborate maze. She'd spent long hours planting the blue delphiniums and now they'd have to be destroyed. It was days like this that made her long to return to her native Ireland.

Her parents had marveled at her knack for growing things in their small village. But due to ever-rising taxes, they lost their moderately successful grocery business, then their home, and then everything else. Paupers, they sent her to England to start a new life. Not long after, the Plague mercilessly ran through their village, taking her parents and nearly everyone else. As a result, Rosaleen had no real family and the long hours she spent toiling in the royal garden meant she had no time for a social life. Besides, a simple, hard-working country girl wasn't meant for the high society of haughty London. A weed among the gilded flowers, she fancied herself. So instead, she devoted all her attention and nurturing to her plants. It turned her stomach that she'd have to rip out the majestic blue delphiniums she'd worked so hard to procure and cultivate.

Unfortunately, this wasn't the first time the royal family had made unreasonable requests of her. That wife King Charles was fond of avoiding, Catherine of Braganza, was often changing her mind as to the placement of various garden features, such as fountains and trellises. This was compounded by the fact that the queen understood little about horticulture.

"I would like a place to sit in the shade and eat apricots," she'd say one day.

"But your majesty," Rosaleen would reply, "apricots are difficult to grow in England. Perhaps a plum or cherry tree might be better suited to the cooler climate."

But the queen would insist. "Apricots complement my olive skin and dark hair. See that it is done."

So Rosaleen would create a charming, secluded area, fashioned with a hand-carved bench and a canopy of apricot trees, laden with supple fruit and defying the natural elements of England's foggy summers. And as soon as she had completed this nearly impossible task, Queen Catherine would decide she preferred the blossoms of the cherry tree to those of apricots, and Rosaleen would begrudgingly start all over again.

She pulled out her pruning shears again and caught sight of her hands. Her nailbeds were lined with dirt and her palms were quilted with calluses.

One of these days I'll remember to put on my gardening gloves.

Knowing there was no time to waste, she ventured to the far end of the garden to begin pulling out the delphiniums. She passed a cluster of rose bushes, both red and white to represent England's symbolic Tudor rose, the emblem of houses united in marriage and harmony. Those rose bushes required exceptional upkeep to maintain their design, color, and arrangement, and Rosaleen dreaded spending time on them each day.

She much preferred the wee, wild roses that freely grew along the Irish countryside, poking up along fence lines or tumbling over walls to greet passersby. Sadly, they were fragile. Once plucked, they did not survive, unlike their English counterparts, which could last up to a week in a vase. That, Rosaleen found, was the most endearing quality of her country's native flora. They were at once hardy enough to grow just about anywhere, in imperfect conditions, yet entirely fragile once disrupted. One learned to appreciate their beauty for what it was.

Just after she passed the Tudor rose cluster, she came to a low spot in the garden, which was often pooled with water. There, her eyes fell on a small rose bush popping up out of the soil. No more than the height of an ant hill, it stood proudly, its blooms stretching toward the sun directly overhead.

"What are you doing here?" she asked aloud, noting its tiny, dark pink flowers. She looked back at the red and white roses, wondering if this variety had been the result of accidental cross-pollination. She pulled out her pruning shears and snipped a perfect rose bud. As she leaned in to admire it, a sharp thorn pierced her thumb, producing a single drop of blood. She felt woozy at first, then cold, and finally unsettled in a way she couldn't describe. As if something inside her had changed.

"Ma'am," a voice called from the other side of the garden's iron gates. "Ma'am, if you please."

Rosaleen shook her thumb, then turned and saw a man with a small girl, faces both smudged, their clothing torn, hair matted.

"Ma'am," he repeated, eyes focused on the ground below his poorly shod feet.

"Yes," Rosaleen said, approaching the gate. "You're new here, aren't you?"

The man's face flushed, and he stood silently, his arm around the shoulder of the girl clinging to his leg. The beggars had been showing up for weeks, peeking through the iron gates to look at the garden and ask for scraps. And yet at the other end of the property, the king, the queen, and their court feasted on lavish meals without a care for those who milled about beyond their walls.

"I'll see what I have," Rosaleen assured.

She took a quick jaunt along the rows of vegetables and fruits, picking a few tomatoes, a bunch of sorrel, and a handful of blackberries. She removed the broad-brimmed straw hat she'd been wearing and dumped it all inside. Then she dug up a few potatoes and headed back to the gate.

"Wait," she said, turning back and making a beeline for her majesty's discarded apricot tree. She plucked the plumpest, juiciest fruits from the tree and dropped them into her hat.

"Here," she said, squatting down and handing the little girl the largest apricot. "This is for you."

Without a word, she reached her grubby hand through the wrought iron bars and snatched the fruit. Rosaleen stood up and held out her hat so the man could take the rest of the produce, which he promptly stuffed in his pockets.

"Thank you, ma'am," he said, bowing repeatedly. "I regret that I'm unable to repay you for your kindness."

"You're welcome. But there is something you could do for me," Rosaleen assured.

The girl was halfway through the apricot by now, a dribble of juice collecting on her dirty chin. "Yes, ma'am," the man said. "What can I do?"

Rosaleen held out the dark pink rose and trimmed off the thorns. Then she handed it to the man. "Go plant this somewhere so that it can be seen by everyone in London. Not just those who have the privilege of frequenting this garden. Something this beautiful deserves to be appreciated by everyone."

{ 3 }

CHAPTER THREE

Goldie snuggled into the space between Minty and Belle on the overstuffed couch in the observatory. She'd been sleeping up here the last few nights, ever since they'd arrived in Epping. Each night, Snowy and Minty had shown her different constellations and celestial objects through the telescope. Goldie tried to remember all the names but was often distracted by Galileo, who liked to cuddle up in her lap.

Tonight, they were having a fancy slumber party with Camille and Annelise.

"After being on a ship with all those men for so long, let's have some girl time," Snowy had said earlier in the day.

"I don't know how you managed to be on a ship with all those stinky boys," Camille piped up.

"Oh, they're not *all* stinky," Minty giggled as she and Snowy exchanged a glance.

"But there are so many of them," Annelise pointed out. "Don't you get tired of being around them all the time?"

Goldie didn't think it was so bad; she really liked Clem and Carter, and the crew had been nice to her. She was comfortable on the ship and had spent time on it each of the past few days, looking around and learning new ways to tie knots and use the different instruments. But tonight was a special night for "the ladies," as Carter referred to them. For the occasion, Minty had made savory hand pies and a rhubarb crumble, and Snowy and Claudette had made popcorn. Everyone sat in their pajamas, brushing each other's hair and sipping valerian root tea.

"Did you know this telescope is the reason we found you in Bonn?" Minty asked, changing the subject.

"You mean you could see her all the way from here?" Belle asked.

"No, silly," Snowy said with a laugh. "When it arrived from Mr. von Brock's factory, it had Goldie's secret message on the lens. I couldn't get it to fit and when I took it apart to see what the problem was, we found the note."

"And then you came to rescue me!" Goldie squealed. "We hooked up the pigs to the carts and rode them out of the factory, and then we fried mean Mr. von Brock so he could never hurt another child again."

"That sounds scary!" Belle said.

"It was a little scary, but then it was fun. After that, we went to an island and fought frogmen and met a giant spider, then we escaped in a balloon," Goldie said, standing up on the couch, her tiny legs wobbling as she acted out her story. "And then after we started sailing again, we got pulled under the ocean by mermen and battled sea monsters, and then—"

"Goldie, stop!" Belle said, huddled against Minty. "You're scaring me!"

"Oh, we don't mean to scare you," Snowy said, grabbing a handful of popcorn from the big bowl on the table and passing the bowl to Belle. "In fact, we've had much scarier adventures, now that I think about it."

"You have?" Annelise asked, her eyes wide.

"Like what?" said Camille.

Claudette, who was sitting on the floor, began working on some knitting as Snowy continued.

"Well, let's see," Snowy began, pausing to chew her popcorn.

"Maybe start at the beginning," Minty suggested. "With the ogres."

"Ogres!" Belle buried her face in Minty's side.

"Ogres, right," Snowy said. "I'd nearly forgotten about them. And Captain Savage."

"Who's that?" Camille asked.

"A pirate," Minty replied. "Well, he was."

"Is he dead?" Goldie asked as she scooped up a handful of popcorn and flopped down on the couch.

"No," Snowy said. "We spared him. But he won't ever bother anyone again. He's in prison at Maldon."

"Maldon? Isn't that where Carter's taking the ship?" Goldie asked.

"Yes, it's right at the North Sea, and there's a shipyard there," Minty explained. "But don't worry. Captain Percival Savage isn't going anywhere."

Belle lifted her head and Goldie took her hand.

"Don't be scared," Goldie said. "Let's hear about the ogres."

She looked at Belle as if she were looking in a mirror. They had the same almond-shaped eyes, the same straight black hair, the same warm tone in their skin. When Belle's hand relaxed, Goldie draped her arm over Belle's shoulder. "I bet it's a great story."

"It is," Snowy said. "And don't worry, I'll tell you right now that it's not too scary because we defeated the ogres, too."

"So, they won't bother anyone again?" Belle asked.

"I doubt it," Minty said. "What was that one called? The big one with the yucky teeth?"

"Booger," Snowy said, giggling.

"Booger!" Goldie exclaimed. "Ew!"

They all broke into laughter, even Claudette who dropped her knitting and shook her head.

"He was pretty gross," Snowy recalled. "Those teeth."

"That breath," Minty said.

"His boogers?" Goldie giggled.

"Those, too," Snowy said. "But let's not fault him for that. I'm sure he couldn't help it, being a mean, smelly ogre. Besides, if it hadn't been for him and the rest of the ogres, we wouldn't have wound up with the honey diamond."

"What's that?" Camille asked.

"A gift from an old friend, Queen Luvhoney," Snowy explained. "It allows us to call upon her and any other bees whenever we need help."

"Bees? Yuck," Belle said. "I don't like bees."

"Oh, but bees are very helpful," Minty said. "Yes, they can sting, but only when they're mad. Without bees, we wouldn't have all the beautiful flowers that grow throughout Epping Forest and make it so lovely."

"Bluebells," Snowy offered.

"Honeysuckle, of course," Minty said.

"Roses?" Goldie asked.

"Yes, roses," Snowy said.

"I like roses," Belle said. "I just don't like bees."

"But we need one in order to have the other," Minty explained.

Goldie offered Belle some popcorn and they nibbled for a minute, thinking.

"I guess if you put it that way," Belle said, "they're not too bad."

Goldie squeezed Belle's shoulder. "That's a good attitude," she said.

Then she listened with great delight as Snowy continued to talk about their adventures fighting Captain Savage, sailing into an ice sheet and discovering a magic icicle, working their way through France and Belgium to get to Bonn, blowing up von Brock's factory with methane made from pig poop, breaking the spell of an angry island medicine man to turn frogs back into people, collecting the Vase of Aquarius from the Okeanos, and receiving the Scepter of the Trees from WC Squirrel in the Bavarian Forest.

As Snowy told of the scepter jumping the ship back to Epping, a loud noise came from downstairs.

"What was that?" Belle asked in a shaky voice.

Claudette was already on her feet and making her way to the top of the stairs.

"Wait," Snowy said, "shh. Let's listen."

A second loud noise echoed from below. Goldie could feel Belle shaking so she squeezed her tighter. Galileo arched his back, his tail puffed out to twice its size.

"I'm going down there," Claudette said. "You girls stay here."

But just as she started down the steps, a familiar voice called out.

"Claudette, it's me, Carter. I hope I didn't startle you," he said. "I was trying to be quiet."

"Carter?" Minty said, getting up and walking to the top of the stairs. "What are you doing?"

"Hi, Minty. I'm sorry to disturb you ladies on your special night, but the door was unlocked," he explained.

Goldie squirmed on the couch, suddenly remembering that Snowy had asked her twice to make sure that the door was locked before coming upstairs. But she was so excited about the slumber party that she forgot.

"It's all right, Carter," Snowy said, joining the others at the top of the stairs. "Did you need something?"

"Just wondering if there were any more hand pies," he said sheepishly. "I want to take them back to the ship for a midnight snack."

"I'll get you some," Minty said, heading down the stairs.

"I thought I asked you to lock the door," Snowy said, turning to Goldie.

"You did," she said. "I'm sorry. I just forgot."

"You can't just forget," Snowy said. "The forest can be a dangerous place. We're lucky it was only Carter, but anyone could've walked in. You have to be more careful."

"I will," Goldie said, her cheeks flushing.

As Snowy and Claudette went to get more blankets, Goldie sat with Belle, Camille, and Annelise.

"Are you in trouble?" Annelise asked.

"I don't think so," Goldie said.

"I wouldn't have said anything," Camille added.

"Me neither," said Belle.

"But why wouldn't I tell the truth?" Goldie asked.

"To stay out of trouble," Annelise said.

Goldie shook her head. "You don't understand," she explained. "I don't know why, but I can't lie. I just can't do it."

"Everyone lies sometimes," Camille said.

"No," Goldie said, her voice raising slightly. "I mean, I *can't* lie."

The other girls looked at her, puzzled. Snowy and Claudette came back with the blankets and started handing them out. Soon, Minty came up the stairs, humming to herself.

"Don't worry," she said with a smile, "I locked it when he left."

Goldie yawned, the valerian tea's sleep-inducing properties taking effect. She curled up under the blanket and closed her eyes. All the stories about ogres and pirates and bees had her brain spinning. So instead she tried to calm herself by thinking about something more pleasant.

She was beginning to like it here. The cottage was small, but it was cozy. She'd never had any real family and enjoyed being around people, and a cat, who made her feel safe and loved. But she was also excited to go to London in a couple days. As she drifted off to sleep, she began thinking of living in a larger, fancier home. A palace, to be precise.

***

Snowy helped Claudette put the breakfast dishes away.

"Thank you for including my girls in the slumber party," Claudette said. "I don't know that they've ever had one before."

"My pleasure," Snowy said. "Seems like they had a good time."

"I guess I don't understand why it's called a slumber party, though. With all those stories about ogres and treasure and pirates, I don't know that they slept very much."

Snowy laughed, "After all those pancakes you made this morning, I bet they'll be sleepy soon enough." She looked out the window and saw Camille, Annelise, and Goldie running in a circle around Belle. "Or maybe they'll just wear themselves out playing." She reached for the broom to sweep the floor, but Claudette took it out of her hands.

"I'll do that," she said. "I know you need to get the ship to Maldon today."

"Thank you, Claudette."

"Minty was in here earlier. She seemed a bit distracted," Claudette said, starting to sweep.

Snowy spied Minty on the deck of the *G2*, talking to her first mate. "I think she's sad to say goodbye to Carter, although I don't know why. He said it won't take long to fix the ship once they get to Maldon. And we should only be gone a few days. It's not like they haven't spent more time apart before."

Claudette smiled. "Well, maybe that was before ... I mean, I can see that those two ... well, it's quite sweet."

"I guess," Snowy said. "And then when we get back, we'll need to prepare for our trip to London. I don't even know what to pack."

"What else do you need besides clothes and toiletries?"

Snowy gazed at Carter and Minty, standing close together and obviously wrapped in conversation while the crew readied the ship. It reminded her of how it felt to talk to Lyr. She thought about all the adventures she, Minty, and Carter had endured together and the many interesting souvenirs they'd picked up along the way.

"Gosh, I can't even think," she said, running her hands through her blonde hair. "We have to be prepared for anything. And we won't have the ship, so that means bringing some tools and other things that would normally be available on board."

She let out a deep sigh. So many things to think about and she was afraid she'd forget something important.

Goldie burst through the door, snapping Snowy out of her thoughts.

"We're going to London!" she said, holding up a stick like a baton and traipsing through the cottage's living room. She had a blanket draped around her shoulders like a cape. Camille and Annelise carried the corners, keeping it from touching the floor as they followed Goldie.

"Girls, please don't track in any dirt," Claudette implored. "I've just swept."

"It's your majesty," Goldie said with a giggle. "And these are my ladies in waiting."

"Oh, I beg your pardon, your majesty," Claudette said with a mock curtsy. "*Mesdames.*"

All three girls chuckled at Claudette's silly gesture.

"Where's Belle?" Snowy asked.

"She didn't want to play royal court," Goldie explained, loosening the blanket knotted around her neck. "She said she wanted to look at the roses instead."

Sure enough, crouched down by the little rose bush, Belle was sitting quietly, running her fingers over the petals and occasionally leaning forward to smell the blossoms.

"My cape is too hot," Goldie announced.

"We'll help you remove it, your majesty," Camille said, helping Goldie.

"Hand me your scepter," Annelise said, motioning for Goldie to give her the stick she'd brought inside.

The scepter. We need to get the ship back to Maldon.

"I hate to interrupt, your majesty," Snowy said, "but would you like to say goodbye to the crew before we leave?

"I've already wished them well on their journey," Goldie said, dramatically exhaling as the blanket came off her shoulders. "You may proceed without me."

"Very well, then," Snowy said. Then she turned to Claudette. "Make sure Belle stays here. We shouldn't be too long in Maldon. When we get back, I'll start packing."

"Of course," Claudette said. She walked Snowy to the door and then motioned for Belle to come inside.

Snowy crouched down. "I'll see you in a little while," she said.

Belle stared at her, saying nothing.

"Well, now," Snowy said, standing up, "Minty and I will be back later."

Then she walked to the sail-bridge and climbed aboard. Minty frowned as Snowy crossed the deck.

"Is it time to go already?" Minty asked.

"I'm afraid so," Snowy said. "You have the scepter?"

"It's down in the hold," Carter said. "I didn't want it to get lost."

"Well, let's get it so we can get the ship to Maldon and then get back here," Snowy said.

Without delay, Clem brought it up to the deck, and Snowy took it in her hands as the crew gathered around her.

"So, if I understood WC correctly, we just have to hold onto this and some other piece of wood, and then think about where we want to go," she said.

"Sounds right to me," Minty said. "Everyone, hold onto the rail."

The crew dispersed, each of them putting a hand on the wooden rail that surrounded the ship. Carter put his free arm around Minty and she leaned into his chest.

"Well, I guess we're ready," Snowy said. She held the scepter aloft and closed her eyes. "Take us to Maldon ... please."

With a whoosh, Snowy felt the ship lift into the air, and then just as quickly, it touched down in the shipyard at Maldon. The salty sea air greeted her as scavenging gulls cried overhead.

"Wow," Snowy said, blinking in disbelief. "That is amazing!"

A murmur of astonishment rippled through the crew as they all realized where they were.

"Carter!" called a voice on the ground. "Snowy! Minty!"

Snowy turned and looked at the man standing at the dock. "Mr. Thompson!" she yelled, waving at him.

"What's happened to this ship? And how did you ..."

"I'll explain when I get down there," Carter said.

"Drop the sail-bridge," Minty said.

Thompson met them at the dock with a handful of bewildered shipwrights.

"It's been so long since we put this thing together," he said. "Looks like it's been holding up well."

"Just here for some repairs," Snowy said. "In fact, Minty and I need to get back to Epping. Carter will be in charge while they're here."

Thompson looked around. "Do you need someone to bring a carriage?"

She pointed the scepter. "No, we've got everything we need."

"I'll explain it to you later," Carter assured him. Then he turned to Minty, took her hand and raised a brow. "Remember what I said. About going to London."

Minty blushed and let out a giggle as he kissed her hand. "I'll remember."

Snowy was confused. "What about London?"

"I'll explain it to you later," Minty said, her eyes still locked on Carter. "Bye, Noah."

He waved as Snowy and Minty stood on the dock and held hands. Snowy lifted the scepter again and wished them back to Epping. In moments, they were back at the cottage.

"I can't believe that works," Minty said.

"What did Carter say to you about London?"

"I'll tell you on the way," Minty said coyly. "I need to pack."

"Don't forget the icicle," Snowy said.

"Do you really think we'll need that? Aren't we just visiting the Observatory?"

"You never know," Snowy said. "I like to be prepared."

Minty nodded. "I know. So, what else do you suppose we should bring?"

Snowy stopped on the front porch of the cottage and looked at the empty space in the grass where the ship had been. "I was thinking we might want to take the honey diamond. The scepter, of course."

"What about the Vase of Aquarius?" Minty asked. "Might get thirsty on the way there or back."

"Good idea," Snowy said. "But, how are we going to carry all these things?"

Minty scratched beneath her chin as she thought. "Oh, we have that big trunk from the Duke of Somerset! It's still in my cottage, up in the attic. Do you think that would work?"

"Probably," Snowy said. "We'd just have to empty all the clothes and jewelry out of it."

Belle, Goldie, Camille and Annelise ran by the porch, not even noticing that Minty and Snowy had returned. "Race you!" Goldie yelled as the other girls followed.

"Oh, I don't think that's going to be a problem," Minty said with a laugh. "I think I know a few little girls who would be more than happy to play dress-up while we're gone."

Snowy watched the girls, who had tumbled together in a heap in front of the rose bush. Goldie scooped up a handful of petals from the ground and started sprinkling them over the other girls.

"Weird," Snowy said.

"What? That they'll play dress-up?"

"No," Snowy said. "I just think it's weird how that rose bush popped up out of nowhere. We've never been able to grow roses here before."

{ 4 }

CHAPTER FOUR

Rosaleen picked at the grime beneath her nail beds. Always forgetting to put on her gardening gloves before digging in the soil. Her delicate alabaster rose cameo set against dark green agate glinted in the sunlight. Its black velvet ribbon encircling her neck was heavy and damp with perspiration. She'd been toiling away since early morning, cultivating neat rows of lily of the valley, chosen to replace the blue delphiniums that had drawn the king's ire a week before. Parched, she pulled out her canteen and took a long swig.

The lilies of the valley were delicate and would require diligent care. But at least they were white and could grow to a similar height as the delphiniums she'd just ripped out, fulfilling the king's expressed requirements. Finally, he would be pleased with her work.

She splashed a handful of water on her freckled face and then rubbed some on the back of her neck as she shook her long black hair. Fixing her wide-brimmed straw hat atop her head, she took a last look at the lilies of the valley proudly bordering the reflecting pool. She'd outdone herself, turning this project around in such a short time. Perhaps now she could get back to the boxwood garden maze she'd been neglecting while focused on this task. She'd been eager to finish it but it seemed the royal family was always pulling her away with their unreasonable demands.

A pair of scavengers loped by the iron gates, peeking in as they always did. A man and a woman, with faces pressed between the bars, craned their necks to take in the garden's stunning view. She was used to them by now, snatching a glimpse of her work from beyond the barrier. The park just beyond the garden was frequented by young families, older couples, and those who had nowhere else to go. A veritable cross-section of London's population, to be honest. The occasional pickpocket hid in the recesses of the garden walls, lying in wait for the ladies with parasols taking their morning stroll. By noon, the park was filled with children, playing tag or other games. The folks who humbly asked for scraps usually came by closer to sundown, after the evening meal had been served.

But the constant parade of the best and worst of humankind didn't bother Rosaleen. In Ireland, she'd been happy to cultivate various plants and flowers in public places, giving everyone in her village and even travelers an opportunity to enjoy her work. But here at the palace, the royal family wanted to hoard away all this natural beauty for their own pleasure.

'Tis a shame to keep it locked away behind these walls.

The clatter of striking metal jarred Rosaleen from her thoughts. She looked up to see two boys at the iron gates, chasing a hoop that had crashed against them. With shouts and giggles, they got the hoop upright and rolled it away with their sticks. A smile crossed Rosaleen's face, wistful of their freedom as she watched them race their hoop across the meadow.

With a sigh, she turned and resumed walking among her plants. The tiny rose bush near the Tudor rose display was blooming again. The intoxicating fragrance filled the air as she pulled her trusty clippers from one of her pockets.

"I've no idea where you've come from," she said aloud as she clipped off several buds. "But you sure are a stubborn rogue. I've cut you back twice now and you keep returnin' with blooms galore."

Realizing she was talking to the plants again, which she often did during long days, she looked around. There didn't appear to be anyone in the garden, fortunately. But she heard a rustling near the wrought iron gates.

Probably a pickpocket, she figured, but it seemed a bit late in the day for that.

Clippings in hand, she went to the shed to find a vase. They would look nice on the table of her modest cottage, adjacent to the garden grounds. She began rifling through the shed to find one the right size but stopped when she heard her name.

"ROSALEEN!"

The king. And from his tone, he didn't sound happy.

She hurried out of the shed, leaving the door ajar in her haste.

"Yes, your majesty? I'm back here," she called, hurrying toward the reflecting pond.

Charles II was a tall man, standing 6' 2", with long black hair that cascaded in waves past his shoulders. He had olive skin, inherited from his Italian grandmother, Marie de Medici, and mother, Henrietta Maria, who was half Spanish. Therefore, he stood out among the British aristocracy, having a truly mixed European lineage and a height much taller than the average Englishman. When he was a boy, civil war broke out and his father was exiled. Then-Prince Charles and his brother James, Duke of York, took part in military activities, but were later sent to safety, eventually joining their mother in France. Years later, after his father was executed, and the monarchy was eventually restored, he took his rightful throne. Though he preached forgiveness publicly and was often referred to as the Merry Monarch, deep down he still reserved scorn for those who had revolted against the crown.

"Rosaleen!" he barked. "What is all this?"

His arms flailed at the lilies of the valley, fresh mounds of dirt still deposited in their beds.

"Lily of the valley, your maje—"

"Take them OUT!" he screamed, causing Rosaleen to recoil. An imposing figure, he frightened her when he was angry.

"But your majesty, this is what you asked for," she implored, her voice shaking.

"No, it certainly is not," he screeched.

Rosaleen felt her anger welling up. Green eyes aflame and limbs trembling, she ran her fingers over the handles of her clippers. She gripped them, steadying her shaking hand as she gathered her composure.

"With all due respect, your majesty," she began as calmly as she could, staring him down, "you asked for tall white flowers to replace the blue delphiniums. There are only so many varieties that will endure the full sun in this spot, and therefore lilies of the valley were one of the few options."

"Miss Bramble, lilies of the valley put off an atrocious odor, and furthermore, their delicate flowers might give the impression of a delicate monarch," he snarled as he ripped a handful of the graceful white flowers out of the ground. "You've seen the wretched, ungrateful peasants who traipse past the gate daily, looking in on this garden. I am the King of Great Britain and Ireland. I must be *respected*. Lilies of the valley are not representative of my authority. You will plant something else."

"But your majesty—"

"See that it is done, Rosaleen!" he said, tossing the upended plants at her feet.

As he stalked out of the garden, Rosaleen felt her anger boil over into a rage. Ever since pricking her thumb, she'd had difficulty controlling her temper. She hung her head in defeat. And then like a branch giving way to a gust of London's powerful wind, she snapped. She stomped on the plants, bruising their stems and crushing their bell-shaped flowers until nothing but torn petals and shredded leaves remained.

Larkspur. That would have to do. Tall, white, and no offensive odor. She'd run out of options and resolved to acquire larkspur tomorrow and begin the task of replacing what she'd just destroyed.

Disgusted and out of breath, she scurried back to the shed, hot tears stinging her cheeks.

This job isn't worth my aggravation. My parents meant well to send me here, but I know they wouldn't want me to stay in such a place.

As she entered the shed, she was startled to see someone in the shadows behind one of the doors. Gasping, she jumped back, her nerves already raw.

"Who are you?" she asked, her voice shaking again.

The man was propped against the wall, but he seemed to be of considerable height. He wore a dark cloak, pulled up over his head, with eyes that narrowed into slits as she approached.

"Never mind who I am," he said, motioning with a gloved hand.

Rosaleen's eyes drifted past him and focused on the pitchfork against the shed's wall.

"You won't be needing that," the man said calmly. "I've not come here to harm you."

She took a cautious step forward. "How did you get in?"

"Never mind that, either," he replied in a raspy voice, staving off a cough.

Taking another shaky step, she brushed off a chill and asked, "Then what do you want?"

"Miss Bramble," the man said, "I've merely brought you a gift."

Something about his voice struck a memorable chord. "A ... gift?"

Clutching his cloak to keep it closed, he motioned to a pile of sacks leaning against the potting table. Rosaleen felt her knees knock as she walked toward them.

"Yes," the man said. "A gift. Something to help ... spread your roots."

She turned to ask what he meant, and how he knew her name, but he was gone. Rosaleen looked at the sacks and then at the spot on the wall where the man had been, now shrouded in mist.

"It couldn't ..." She drew her hand to her neck, touching the cameo, then shook her head. "No. Impossible."

{ 5 }

CHAPTER FIVE

Snowy loaded the last of the luggage onto the carriage as dawn broke. It wouldn't take long to get to London, but she wanted to be sure they'd get there before sundown.

"Here," Claudette said, handing her a stack of newspapers. "These piled up while you were gone. I thought you might like to read them along the way. I know those long rides can be boring."

"It has been a while since I read a newspaper," Snowy said, setting the stack on the carriage's seat. "We were gone so long. First in the Caribbean and then under the ocean, and then in Bavaria. It's been hard to keep up. What's the big news here, Claudette? Anything exciting?"

Claudette looked at the ground and clutched her apron. "Well, actually ... I'm not sure," she said quietly. "I can't ..."

Snowy searched Claudette's face, which was creased with shame.

"Oh, Claudette," Snowy said, putting an arm around the woman's shoulders. "If you'd like, I'd be happy to teach you to read when we return. Don't you dare feel bad about that."

Claudette's face collapsed as tears flooded her eyes. "I just never learned. I sent my girls to school and wanted only the best for them, so they could have opportunities I didn't. But I was always working. Especially after my husband died, I was working so much to keep us fed and clothed. I would love to learn. That is, if you don't mind."

Snowy smiled and gave Claudette a squeeze. "I don't mind at all," she said. "Reading is freedom. It takes you to new worlds, whisks you away to exciting adventures, and teaches you things you didn't know that you didn't know. It'll be my privilege to teach you, Claudette."

"Teach Claudette what?" Minty said as she walked up to the carriage, a yawn escaping her lips.

Snowy looked at Claudette, who was dabbing her eyes. "Oh, nothing," she said. "Are you ready to go to London?"

Minty walked over to pet the ponies tethered to the reins. "I suppose," she said. "Just waiting for Goldie to finish her breakfast and say goodbye to Annelise, Camille, and Belle."

"I'm surprised she wasn't out here already," Claudette said with a smile. "It's all she's been talking about since you read the letter from Mr. Flamsteed."

"Pretty sure it's all she's going to talk about the whole way there," Minty said, climbing into the carriage's seat. "Snowy, are you driving, or do you want me to?"

Snowy looked at the newspapers. "Why don't you drive first, and I'll drive after we stop to rest."

"Fine with me," Minty said.

Right on cue, Goldie came racing out to the carriage, with the other girls trailing behind. "I beat you!" she said, clapping her hands with glee.

Claudette scooped up Goldie and kissed her cheek. "You be careful and listen to Snowy and Minty," she said. Then she opened the door to the carriage. "In you go."

"I want to ride on top with Minty!" Goldie cried.

"Goldie," Snowy said, settling into the passenger seat, "there's not enough room up here. Besides, if you get tired, it'll be easier and more comfortable to take a nap back there."

"I'll switch places with you when we get closer to London," Minty offered. "That way you can see all the sights from up here. How does that sound?"

"Alright," Goldie sighed as she climbed into the carriage.

Claudette tucked her in and then closed the door. "Don't worry," she said. "I'll keep everything running smoothly while you're gone."

"I'm not worried about anything," Snowy said with a wink. "I'm confident it's all in capable hands."

Everyone waved as Minty took the reins and they set out to cross Epping Forest on the way to London. As the sun climbed in the sky, Snowy leafed through the newspapers.

"Well, this is interesting," she said. "King Charles II is currently staying at St. James Palace."

"Wasn't he born there?" Minty asked. "I thought he lived in Windsor Castle."

"They're doing some renovations at Windsor," Snowy said, working her way through the article. "And it says that people are enjoying the royal gardens which border St. James Park."

"He lets them in the garden?"

Snowy read further. "I don't think so," she said. "I think they can just walk by and look through the gates."

"Well, that's too bad," Minty said as they crossed the forest's floor, passing moss-covered trees and clusters of foxgloves.

"Right," Snowy said, looking up from the newspaper and taking in the view of the forest. "Not everyone is lucky enough to live near the forest or in a palace. I mean, I know we get to see this all the time. And fancy buildings are pretty architecture are nice. But I'm sure the average Londoner doesn't see a lot of flowers and plants."

"Probably not," Minty said, leading the ponies up a slight incline. "Goldie, how are you doing back there?"

When Minty's question was met with silence, Snowy turned around to look through the little window at the top of the cab. Goldie was snoozing away, her head on a velvet cushion.

"She's asleep," Snowy said, confirming what she'd expected to happen.

"Ahh," Minty said. "Not surprised."

"At least it'll be quiet for a while," Snowy laughed.

They pressed on, chatting and enjoying the scenery as Minty drove. Snowy had seen more of the small rose bushes scattered throughout the forest. Not just pink like the one at the cottage, but yellow, ivory, and red tones, too. "Are you noticing these roses?" she finally asked.

"Yes," Minty replied. "I guess it's a good year for them."

"Must be," Snowy said, looking through the newspaper again. After a while, she said, "Oh, well this is weird. Like Mr. Flamsteed said, there are roses growing all over London. No one seems to know where they've come from."

"That is weird," Minty said. "I wonder what that means."

"Like you said, must be a good year."

Minty clucked her tongue to coax the ponies over a slight ridge. Snowy held on as the carriage shifted along the bumpy path, then felt the breeze go through her hair as they worked their way down the grade. It wasn't quite the same sensation as sailing on the *G2*, but it still felt good to be outside, breathing fresh air.

"I wonder how the repairs are going on the *G2*," she mused.

"Carter didn't think they'd take too long," Minty said. "I'm sure they're going smoothly. Mr. Thompson will be helpful, I'm sure."

"Oh," Snowy said, "I still feel so bad about snapping at him when we were building the *G2*. Remember that? He must've thought I was awful."

"We all grow and change," Minty replied. "I'm sure he's forgiven you by now."

"I'd like to think that. So, what's with you and Carter?"

Minty coughed. "Oh, uh, well ..."

"You don't have to tell me if you don't want to," Snowy assured.

"No, it's fine. I guess, Noah, uh, Carter and I have become fond of each other," she said.

"You're the only one I know who calls him Noah. Even Clem calls him Carter."

"Well, that's his first name," Minty said. Then she smiled. "I'm still trying to find out his middle name."

Snowy laughed. "He hasn't told you?"

"No, he said it's a secret."

Snowy laughed louder. "Oh, we're going to find out."

They chuckled as the carriage continued through the forest. The sunlight was warming their faces, but Goldie continued to snooze. Snowy flipped through another newspaper, reading about growing discontent among the British citizens opposed to the high taxes imposed by the monarchy.

Some things never change.

Then her eye landed on an article about a small orphanage in one of London's impoverished neighborhoods. It said that four children had died and at least six others had fallen ill.

"Oh, this is terrible," Snowy said.

"What is?" Minty asked.

"It says that several children at the Hitchcock House for London Youth have become ill, and no one seems to know why."

"The Hitchcock House, that sounds familiar, doesn't it?"

"I think it's not too far from the Observatory," Snowy recalled. "Says here it's in the Rosemary Lane neighborhood. Near Kew Gardens and not too far from the Thames."

"That sounds right," Minty said. "Does it say what they think it might be that's making everyone sick?"

Snowy read more of the article. "No, not really. Just that there have been four deaths, three girls and a boy, and that at least six other children are sick. Respiratory problems that just got worse and then they died."

"Sounds awful," Minty said. "Those poor children."

"I know," Snowy said, folding the paper and setting it aside. "I mean, think about Goldie, and all the other children from the orphanage in Epping. That's a hard enough life as it is. I can't imagine how much harder it would be to get sick and not have your family around to take care of you."

Minty and Snowy sat in silence for a while, contemplating the sadness of it all, and the carriage rolled on toward London.

***

Minty pulled the reins to direct the ponies to a shady spot. They had been heading south all morning and were about to turn and head west toward London. But first, they needed to rest, get some food and water for themselves and the ponies, and prepare for the final leg of their journey. Besides, Goldie had been yammering for the last hour and it would be good for her to stretch her legs and burn off some energy. And, there was a stream nearby, so they'd be able to get fresh water.

"Whoa!" Minty called as the ponies pulled to a stop beneath a large ash tree, just near the entrance to a village. The gray-brown bark was set off by a canopy of bright green leaves cascading down the branches. About forty yards beyond the tree was a stone marker that read Stratford, and then just past that, a gabled arch of stacked stones. Minty could see several half-timbered buildings beyond the village's entrance, lining the cobbled streets.

"Are we there yet?" Goldie sighed dramatically as she flung open the carriage door.

Snowy looked at Minty and offered a weak smile.

"Not yet," Minty said, unhitching the ponies and tethering them to the other side of the tree. "We're going to rest for a bit and then Snowy's going to take her turn driving the carriage."

"Then I get to ride on top!" Goldie squealed, clapping her hands.

"Well, not yet," Snowy said as she pulled a picnic basket and blanket from the carriage. "It's safer for you to stay inside for now. But I promise I'll stop just before we get to London so you can see everything. But for now, let's set up our picnic back here by the stream so the horses can have some space."

Snowy and Goldie walked to a smaller group of trees set off the road and spread out the blanket. Meanwhile, Minty pulled some carrots out of the carriage and went around to feed the ponies. They happily munched on the treats in her hands, and she petted their muzzles and ran her fingers through their manes, telling them what a good job they'd done getting them this far.

"Oh, I forgot your water," Minty said. As she turned to walk back to the carriage, she plowed straight into something—or someone—solid, knocking her to the ground.

"OH, I do beg your pardon, Miss," a husky voice said.

Minty blinked, somewhat disoriented, and focused on a hand stretched toward her. There was grease below the nailbeds, and the fingers were rough, covered in nicks and scratches. With her eyes, she followed the hand to an arm and the arm to a face, which was smudged with something black and warmed by a wide, youthful grin. Gentle brown eyes greeted her below a shock of thick, dark hair, barely contained by a short-brimmed cap.

"Miss?" the young man repeated, bobbing his hand toward Minty. "I do apologize. I'd only come to 'ave a look at your 'orses. Please, let me 'elp you to your feet."

She shook her head and took his hand. "Thank you," she managed as she stood up and dusted herself off.

Immediately, he removed his cap and bent over in a showy bow. His hair, wild and curly, tumbled over his face, stretching every which way. His trousers were covered in so many patches, it was impossible to tell where the trousers ended and the patches began. In fact, they seemed more like a collection of patches held together by trousers instead of the other way around. "Again, I offer me sincerest of apologies," he said, still holding her hand. "Name's Freddie. Freddie Highbolt."

"Minty," she said.

"What's minty?" He donned his cap again and put his hand up to his mouth and sniffed. "Me breath, is it?"

"No," she said with a laugh, noticing that in fact, he smelled like dust and sweat. "That's my name. Minty."

"Oh," he said. "Quite extraordinary, that name, Minty. But then, I suppose it suits you. If I may say, you seem to be quite an extraordinary lass."

Minty pushed her auburn locks behind her ear. "What does that mean?"

"Extraordinary? It means you're not the ordinary type."

"I *know* that—"

"But come to think of it, that's an odd word, now innit? Extraordinary. If something, or in this case, *someone*, is extraordinary, wouldn't it mean they're *extra* ordinary? As in, even more ordinary than average? The most ordinary sort of ordinary? Because that doesn't describe you at all, Miss Minty."

Her green eyes searched his earnest face as she struggled to come up with a response. Then they focused on his toned, muscular frame, stretching taut the dark fabric of his shirt and patched pants. Though he had boyish features, he was clearly a man. The leanness of his frame only emphasized his sculpted physique.

"Well," she stammered, "I don't know about that."

He smiled, relaxing his posture, and Minty felt herself relax as well. "Ah, me and me big ol' reckless gob. 'ow I do go on. I didn't mean to embarrass you. Maybe I should start over. Let's see. Ah, yes. 'ello." He put his hand out. "My name's Freddie Highbolt. Pleased to make your acquaintance."

She returned his handshake with a firm grip. "My name's Minty. The pleasure is mine, Freddie."

"That's more like it," he said, giving her hand a light squeeze before releasing it. "Can I take a wee look at your 'orses, Miss Minty?"

"Of course," she said, leading him around the other side of the tree and taking a bucket from the side of the carriage, where he patted the ponies and stroked their manes. "But I do need to get them some water. We've had a long morning."

"Oh, allow me to help you fetch that," he said, taking the bucket from her hands as they walked toward the stream. "Where ya 'eaded today?"

"To London," she said. "We're going to the Royal Observatory to meet John Flamsteed."

"Ah, I see," he said. "You're a city girl, are ya? The Royal Observa'try, that's 'igh livin'."

"No," Minty said. "We're from Epping. Just here for a visit."

He dipped the bucket into the water and let it fill. "So just a country lass, then, is it? Well, I 'ope you'll enjoy your stay. Me pops and me, we've got business in London, go there most days of the week."

"What kind of business?" They started back toward the tree where the ponies were tethered.

"We're chimbleys," he said.

Minty stopped on the creek bank and stared blankly at the mention of this unfamiliar term.

"You know, chimney sweepers. I 'elp with the family business. Got four little sisters at home, plus me mum, but she can't work on account of her scarlet fever. Me da' is off on business most nights lately—got a new boss who's a real tyrant, it seems. Runs a tight ship, but 'e pays in shiny gold coins. So I keep things going during the day to fill the coffers, else we'd never survive, I'm afraid. The royals 'ave made it so bloody 'ard—oh, pardon me French, Miss—the royals 'ave made it awfully difficult to keep a workin' class family fed. Meanwhile, they're stuffed up in their fancy castles all day, 'avin' their fancy masquerade balls and whatnot, and 'oardin' all the wealth to themselves while us commoners rot in the streets. But it's al'right. We're a plucky bunch."

Minty was infatuated with his roguish speech, unpolished charm, and strong, youthful appearance. But something struck her as odd about his story.

"Why does your father sweep chimneys at night?"

"Minty!" Goldie yelled, waving as she got up and ran toward them, with Snowy following.

"Oh," she said, "would you like to meet my friends?"

"Appears I don't 'ave a choice, 'ey?"

"Snowy, Goldie, this is Freddie," Minty said as they approached. "We, uh—"

"We just ran into each other," Freddie said, exchanging a knowing smile with Minty. "As luck and circumstances would 'ave it."

"Hello," Snowy said, extending her hand. "I'm Snowy."

"Miss Snowy," he said, removing his cap and shaking her hand. Again, his thick curls tumbled over his brow. Then he crouched down and reached behind Goldie's ear, pulling out a shiny coin. "And what's all this then?"

"How did you do that?" Goldie squeaked as he gave her the coin.

"That's a gift for you, Miss Goldie," he said, patting her head as he stood up.

"Wow! Thank you!"

"You're very welcome, Miss Goldie. You be sure to 'ang on to that, in case you ever need it. Never know when it might get you out of a pinch."

"I will!" She stuffed the coin in the pocket of her dress and then ran back to the blanket still spread out near the stream.

"I should look after her," Snowy said. "Nice to meet you, Freddie."

"Miss," he said, doffing his cap once more.

As they walked back toward the horses, Minty said, "So you're in London most of the week?"

"Right, right," Freddie said, holding out the bucket for each of the ponies to drink. "Lots of 'ouses with chimneys there. Lots of work."

"Freddie!" a harsh voice called. "Let's go!"

Minty turned and saw a man in dark clothes with a cap like Freddie's, standing just on the other side of the stone arch. He waved his arm, beckoning.

"Ah, that's me da'," he said. "'e worked 'is other job late last night and isn't too chipper today. I best be going. Thanks for the conversation, Miss Minty."

"No, thank you."

"And again, I apologize for knocking you down. Maybe I'll 'ave the good fortune to see you in London," he said.

"I'd like that," Minty said, her pulse elevating as she noticed his dimples.

All those muscles and dimples, too?

"Freddie! NOW!"

Minty jumped at Freddie's father's gruff tone. But Freddie barely flinched.

"'right, then, off I go. Safe travels."

"You too," she said, then she watched him hurry off to meet his father.

Just as he crossed under the arch, Freddie's father smacked him in the arm and gave him a shove. Minty cocked her head, wondering if everything was all right. It seemed an odd way for a father to treat his son, but sometimes things aren't what they seem.

As Minty walked back to her friends. Goldie held her coin up to the sun, letting it shimmer.

"Is that a doubloon?" Snowy asked, taking a closer look.

Goldie shrugged.

Minty examined it. "I haven't seen one of those for a while. I guess they're circulating even in London now."

"I bet you're hungry," Snowy said, handing her a small parcel wrapped in brown paper. "I brought you a sandwich."

"Thanks," Minty said, tearing into it as she watched Freddie and his father walk down the village's cobble street. "I'm starving."

"He seems nice," Snowy said. Then she started talking about how long it would take to get to London. "Minty?"

"Huh? What? Sorry," she said.

Snowy laughed. "Come on," she said. "When you're done eating, we'll get back in the carriage. We should be in London in an hour or so."

"Uh-huh." Minty kept watching until they were out of sight, barely hearing anything Snowy said. "Extraordinary."

CHAPTER SIX

Snowy gazed into the distance as the carriage followed the River Lea, heading toward the Royal Observatory. The half-timber buildings and cobblestone streets of Stratford were behind them now. London awaited. The Lea would take them through Bromley and down to the Thames. They'd be able to cross over by way of bridge, and then descend into Greenwich, the section of London that was home to the Observatory. But for now, she was enjoying the pastoral views and the scent of England's fragrant summer blooms along the path.

Minty had been quiet since they left Stratford, other than the occasional brief comment or short, polite answer. Usually when they went somewhere, they passed the driving time by talking about all sorts of things like constellations and savory scone recipes. But there was a noticeable change in Minty's demeanor now.

"So," Snowy said, breaking the silence, "tell me about meeting Freddie. He said you ran into each other?"

Minty smiled. "Actually, I ran into him," she explained. "I was feeding the ponies. Turned around to get the water bucket and walked right into that big, broad chest."

"Chest?"

Minty blushed. "I guess I never heard him walk up," she said. "The ponies were crunching their carrots and I didn't know he was standing there and then, uh, we sort of collided and I fell back."

"Ouch, are you all right?"

"Fine. It didn't hurt. And he helped me up," Minty said.

"Well, that was nice of him."

"Yes, he's very polite." A little smile crossed her lips and then she turned her head away.

"I see," Snowy said, wondering what that might be about. She started to ask, then thought better of it. "The flowers are so pretty over there," she said, pointing to a mound of stately yellow irises and delicate cross-leaved heath just off the path. Encircling them was a vine with several pale pink rosebuds.

Minty nodded, still lost in her daydream, it appeared.

After crossing the bridge to take them to Greenwich, Snowy pulled over to the side of the path. "Goldie," she said, "it's time. Come on up here."

Minty stepped down from the carriage and hoisted Goldie into the seat.

"Listen to Snowy, little one," she said, helping her get settled. "And be sure to hold on tight."

"I will," Goldie promised as Minty climbed in the back.

As soon as Snowy got the carriage moving, Goldie peppered her with questions about London. She answered as many as she could, more focused on the road, which was beginning to fill with other travelers as they neared the city.

They journeyed through the outskirts of Greenwich, passing several rundown buildings with dirty water pooled up along the road. Though the buildings were in disrepair, Snowy noted that there were several rose bushes dotting the route, which was beginning to shift from a dirt path to cobblestones. Among the dirt and grime, the thick fragrance of roses soothed Snowy's senses. Goldie delighted in the little shop windows and the mix of people strolling the streets. A study in the city's working class, Snowy spotted sailors, washer women, chimney sweeps, hackney carriage drivers, fishmongers, and the like. As they entered the thick of the city and streets became more numerous, clusters of children in shabby clothes walked together in packs.

"Goldie," Snowy warned, "stay close to me."

Before long, they entered another wooded area.

"Are we still in the city?" Goldie asked.

"Yes, we're in Greenwich," Snowy replied.

"What happened to London?"

"Greenwich is part of London," Snowy explained. "The east end. You'll see where we're going soon."

"Look at the roses!" Goldie said, pointing to a series of bushes along the route.

"Yes, Greenwich is still a wooded area," Snowy said. "There are lots of trees and flowers here. You almost forget that you're in a city."

Snowy steered the ponies up a slope, and as they came to a clearing, the Observatory's brick walls greeted them.

"Wow!" Goldie said. "Is that where we're going?"

"Yes, our friend John Flamsteed lives there," Snowy said. "We'll be staying at the Observatory while we visit."

"It's so big," Goldie gasped.

"Wait until you see the inside. You'll love it."

Goldie clapped her hands as they made their way up the hill. Finally, they came to a stop outside the brick building. Within moments, John Flamsteed appeared with the Duke of Somerset following behind him.

"Hello!" he called. "So good to see you!"

As he offered Snowy his hand to step down from the carriage seat, Somerset opened the door and helped Minty out. The four of them embraced and then Snowy turned to retrieve Goldie.

"This is our friend, Goldie," she said.

"Oh, Miss Goldie," said Flamsteed, crouching down to shake the little girl's hand. "You're the one we heard so much about. Rescued from the telescope factory in Bonn with that dreadful Heinrich von Brock. I'm so glad you're safe now. It's a pleasure to make your acquaintance."

"And Minty, look at how you and Snowy have grown since we last saw you," the duke said, taking a step back. "I dare say, with all respect, the two of you have grown into such lovely young ladies. Your adventurous travels have surely treated you well."

"Well," Snowy said, "they've been adventurous, that's for sure."

A small staff emerged from the Observatory and began unloading the carriage.

"Set them up in the guest quarters," Flamsteed instructed. "We'll be taking our tea shortly."

With that, he led everyone inside.

"It's so kind of you to allow us to stay here, Mr. Flamsteed," Snowy said. "We certainly appreciate the hospitality."

"Well, as you know, as Astronomer Royal, I live here with my family. However, they're currently away visiting my in-laws, so there's plenty of room for the three of you. Please, make yourselves at home."

"Will Sir Wren be joining us?" Minty asked.

"I'm afraid not," the duke replied. "As you know, he designed this building and he has been working on rebuilding St. Paul's Cathedral since it was destroyed in the Great Fire in 1666. He's doing some work there right now, as well as a new library at Trinity College."

"In Cambridge?" Snowy asked, her blue eyes widening.

"Yes," Flamsteed said. "He's been away for a while. I don't expect he'll be back right away, unfortunately. But he does send his regards."

They crossed the Octagon Room and Goldie gasped. Her eyes fixed on the wood paneled walls, topped with pediments and oversized portraits, interrupted only by tall windows that framed the beautiful gardens outside. A table was set in the middle of the room, and a tea cart waited nearby.

"Shall we?" Flamsteed said, motioning to the table. "I'm sure you'd enjoy some refreshments after your long journey. And we can't wait to hear all about your recent adventures."

Snowy took a seat across from a tall window, giving her a clear view into the garden. It felt good to sit and enjoy something nice to eat and drink. After so many adventures, simple things seemed like luxuries. The five of them sat for nearly two hours, talking about the rescue at the telescope factory, the trip to the Caribbean, their voyage below the sea, and finally their experiences in Bavaria, helping WC Squirrel and his friends.

"I must say, it all sounds fascinating," Flamsteed said.

"Indeed," the duke added.

Something outside caught Snowy's eye, causing her to squint, even with her glasses on.

"Miss Snowy?" Flamsteed asked. "Is everything all right?"

"Can we go out to the gardens? I'd like to take a look at something."

"Of course we can," Flamsteed said, getting up from the table. "I think a bit of fresh air is in order, especially on such a lovely day as this."

"Mr. Flamsteed," Snowy said as they went to the door, "in your letter you said that the king was falling out of favor with the English citizens. Why do you suppose that is?"

The duke held the door open for everyone and they filed out.

"Oh, I suppose the most common reason is the same one that beleaguers every monarch. People feel that the rich hold onto too much wealth, leaving an insufficient amount for everyone else."

They stepped onto a path that led between two meticulously groomed lawns, then gave way to various planter boxes filled with fruits, vegetables, and flowers. Snowy felt like she could smell the sunlight, strewn across on the leaves of the plants and warming the plump fruits ready to be picked. Bees buzzed and little white butterflies flitted about as they continued across the garden.

"Well," Minty said, "that's probably a valid complaint."

The duke nodded in agreement as he helped Goldie navigate a tomato cage along the path.

"I wanted to ask you about this rose bush," Snowy said, stopping suddenly. "Has it always been here?"

Flamsteed looked down at the small bush with the dark pink flowers. "It's funny that you ask," he said. "To be honest, I don't recall that being here before. You see, we generally keep vegetables and fruits in this part of the garden, and flowers grow up ahead, as you can see. I suppose we had a little help from the birds."

Snowy squatted down to get a closer look, adjusting her glasses.

"But now that you mention it," Flamsteed continued, "it's highly unusual for roses to grow here."

"Why's that?" Minty asked.

"Well, being so close to the Thames, which is just north of us, this soil is often too damp for roses," he explained. "But it is quite lovely. And fragrant. The birds have done us a favor."

Snowy squinted at the rose bush and carefully ran her fingers down the base, avoiding the large, spiky thorns jutting from it. She grasped it and tugged back and forth. For only being there a short time, it seemed that the roots had taken hold quite well. Then she pulled a small glass vial from her pocket and uncorked it.

"What's that?" Goldie asked.

"Something I keep on me for special occasions," Snowy said, scooping some of the soil up with her free hand. Then she carefully funneled it into the vial, replaced the cork, and tucked it back into her pocket. She held it up, scrutinizing the soil sample.

"Interesting," she said.

***

Minty splashed her face with fresh water from the porcelain bowl in one of the Observatory's apartments. It had been a long day, and the cool water soothed her skin. She dabbed at her face with a thick towel and set it on the mahogany dressing table. Peering into the large, round swivel mirror atop the table, she smoothed her auburn hair away from her face. The day in the sunlight had brought out her freckles, but she knew there was another reason for her golden glow.

Freddie.

While Snowy was going on about battling frogmen and diving under the ocean to take on evil mermen, Minty's mind had been elsewhere. In the shade of an ash tree, charmed by Freddie's wide smile and manly build, to be exact. She wondered if she'd be lucky enough to see him again while they were in London.

"Hey," said a voice from the doorway.

Minty jumped and then turned to see Snowy.

"You all right? I knocked twice."

"Oh," Minty said, steadying her pulse. "I guess I didn't hear you. Sorry."

Snowy scrunched her face. "It's fine. Goldie wants to go out and see the big city, as she keeps calling it. Mr. Flamsteed needs to do some work, but I thought the three of us could take the carriage and ride around a bit before dinner?"

"Sure," Minty said. "Give me a few minutes and I'll be ready."

Snowy closed the door and Minty went back to the dressing table to brush her hair. Then she changed into a clean green dress, one that didn't smell like she'd been riding down dusty paths and cobblestone streets all day. At last, she swooped up the hair around her face and tied it back with a ribbon. She looked into the mirror and smiled, feeling as fresh as a morning bloom.

Outside the Observatory, the duke helped the girls to the carriage. "I'm sorry I can't go along and chaperone," he said. "I've some business to handle as well. But I'll be back later to join you ladies for dinner. Do enjoy your foray into London."

"Any particular places you'd recommend we visit since we only have a few hours?" Snowy asked as she took the reins. Goldie wiggled on the seat next to her.

The duke secured the carriage door as Minty sat inside. "From here, I'd say St. James Park is a good option. It's adjacent to St. James

Palace and it has lovely gardens. There's a wall around them, but you can see through the gates. It's also a wonderful place for people watching if you enjoy that sort of thing. Londoners and visitors come from all over to stroll in the park."

"That sounds perfect," Snowy said. "Goldie, what do you think?"

"To the park!" she said, her forearm aloft.

"I guess it's decided, then," Snowy said.

"Head west and you'll find the road," the duke advised. "Should only take about twenty minutes to get there. Cross the Thames near Stockwell and then it's just ahead, past Westminster Abbey."

"Ooh!" Goldie clapped her hands excitedly.

"Got it," Snowy said, tugging the reins to get the ponies moving.

"Thank you," Minty said, poking her head out of the carriage and waving goodbye as they pulled away. It was nice to sit in the back and stretch out her legs. She closed her eyes and tuned out the million questions Goldie was asking Snowy as they headed westward from the Observatory. Within minutes, she was asleep, lulled by the gentle gait of the ponies as they bobbed along the path.

The scent of roses on a late summer breeze woke her up. It filled her head as she opened her eyes. Outside the carriage, Minty could see rosebushes dotting the riverbank as clusters of people walked by. A large green lawn sprawled ahead. Snowy steered the carriage to a hitching post and Minty got out and then helped Goldie off the front seat.

"It's so pretty!" the child said. "And there's so much room to run! Race you!"

Without warning, she took off, dashing across the grass.

"Goldie!" Minty called as she ran after her. "Slow down!"

Giggling and squealing, Goldie barreled down a hill, with Minty giving chase as Snowy finished at the hitching post. But soon Goldie's little legs couldn't keep up with her momentum and she began to stumble, hurtling toward a group of people.

"Goldie! Look out!" Minty yelled.

Just as the little girl began to fall, a young man spun around and grabbed her around the waist, lifting her into the air.

Minty hurried down the hill, being careful not to slip but eager to thank him for his good deed.

"Well, 'ello again," he said.

Winded, Minty relaxed when she saw that easy smile on Freddie's face.

"Hello," she said, almost breathless as she pulled Goldie from his hands and set her on the grass. "Thank you so much. That could've ended terribly."

Snowy had come up behind them, a stern look creasing her face. "Goldie, you cannot just run off like that. You could've been hurt or hurt someone else. It's a good thing Freddie was here."

Goldie lowered her head and started to cry. "I'm sorry," she sobbed. "I was so excited. Please don't be mad at me."

Minty started to reach for Goldie, but Freddie put his hand up, halting her, as he crouched down.

"Miss Goldie," he said, gently stroking her hair, "no one is mad at you. You're a child and you're full of wonder and imagination and all sorts of rambunctious energy, 'ey?"

The little girl nodded, sniffing away her tears.

"Right, so it's fine to 'ave all that energy. You just need to be careful that your energy doesn't crash into someone else."

Minty watched as Goldie threw her arms around Freddie's neck and hugged him.

"Oh, what's all this then?" he said, patting her back.

"I'm embarrassed," she said quietly.

"There, there, it's alright. It can be 'ard to control our energy. But don't ever be embarrassed by it," he said, standing up. "Then again, sometimes crashing into someone else isn't all that bad, now is it?"

Minty smiled, thinking about their earlier encounter.

"Goldie, why don't you hold my hand and we can walk on the path," Snowy said.

"What are you doing here?" Minty asked as Snowy and Goldie began to walk away.

"I could ask you the same," Freddie replied.

"We had tea earlier at the Observatory and now we're just getting some fresh air before we head back for dinner in a couple hours."

"Tea at the Royal Observat'ry?" Freddie said, dramatically clutching his chest. "My, my, Miss Minty, I reckon you do mingle in such 'igh circles. Probably can't be bothered being seen with someone such as meself, with me tattered pants and me face all smudged with soot."

She rolled her eyes. "Don't be silly," she said, shaking her head. "That doesn't bother me at all."

There was that wide smile again. "Well, then," he said, offering her his arm, "fancy a walkabout?"

She slipped her hand inside the crook of his elbow and they set off behind Snowy and Goldie. Minty felt her pulse accelerate but the soothing scent of blooming flowers helped her relax. She could see that Snowy and Goldie were already walking up to the wrought iron gate.

"Oh, the duke told us we'd enjoy the gardens here," she said.

"The duke?" he began. "Ah, I won't even ask. But 'oever 'e is, 'e's right. The royal gardens are quite the attraction. Would you like to take a gander?"

"Yes," she said as he led her to the path.

They looked inside and Minty saw a woman in a dark green shirt and trousers, her face shaded by a broad-brimmed hat. She dug her bare hands into the earth, carefully placing a small, leafy plant deep inside the hole, then lovingly patted the soil around it.

Everywhere she looked, Minty saw beautiful blossoms in every color imaginable. Trees laden with juicy fruits shaded the paths and a carefully groomed hedge wound through the far corner like a labyrinth. Just at the edge of her view, Minty could see a stunning fountain.

"Wow," she said under her breath. "I've never seen anything so pretty."

"I 'ave," he said, causing her to turn and hold his gaze. He put his rough hand beneath her chin and Minty felt her pulse flutter again. Then he suddenly spun around. "'Ey, move on!" he yelled at two skinny youths who were standing behind Snowy and Goldie. "You 'eard me, go!"

Snowy and Goldie whipped around to see the two young men scamper off.

"Bleedin' pickpockets," Freddie said, his face tense. "The Blackguard. They run rampant in this area, but usually not until nightfall. You ladies al'right?"

Snowy and Goldie nodded, looking a bit flustered.

"They won't 'arm you," Freddie said. "Not while I'm around, anyway."

Minty caught her breath as he puffed out his chest.

"Thank you," Snowy said, holding Goldie's hand tightly.

"Just mind yourselves," he said, brushing it off.

"Why do they do that?" Minty asked.

Freddie turned to her. "To be 'onest, I understand. Just tryin' to survive. The Crown's not been too kindly to the workin' class, as I said earlier. And now we've got sickness breaking out again, people going without clean water when they can't even afford a decent meal."

"No clean water?" Minty asked.

"Right, in the poor neighborhoods," Freddie explained, "like Rosemary Lane, and Bromley. Seems workin' people can't catch a break. It's a shambles, really."

"Rosemary Lane," Minty said. "We read something in the newspaper about that area. An orphanage?"

"Right, right," Freddie nodded. "Pity what's 'appened there. All those children, ill because the Crown doesn't do enough to protect its citizens."

They stood in silence for a moment and then Freddie said, "Well, I 'ate to do it, but I need to get back to work. I'm glad I got to see you again."

"Likewise," Minty said. "Thank you."

He held out his hand. When she took it, instead of a handshake, he lifted it to his lips for a soft kiss.

"My pleasure, Miss Minty," he said. "Until we meet again."

She stood and watched as he walked away, barely hearing Snowy come up behind her.

"He sure is charming," she said. "But what about Noah?"

Minty turned and looked at Snowy. "Who?"

CHAPTER SEVEN

Rosaleen mopped her brow with the back of her soil-stained hand, exhausted from planting all the larkspur. Hunched over a cluster of lavender, she trimmed the spiky stems jutting into the garden's path. The herb's soft, medicinal scent suggested a long, soothing soak in the tub, one of the few indulgences Rosaleen allowed herself after working for hours in the elements. It had been a long day and now the sun was beginning to sink. Soon, the pickpockets would be out and then after that, those who came to the gates to ask for food. She'd already picked a basket of apricots from the queen's neglected grove and set them aside. Then she browsed the overloaded tomato vines and French peas winding up their bamboo trellises, searching for surplus goodies to hand out.

She thought about the Earl of Gloucester, out for an evening stroll with the Marchioness of Nottingham recently, and all those royal brats trailing behind them. How they'd been in the garden, tromping about, with no regard for her carefully cultivated flora. The disrespect for horticulture was bad enough, but the way they sneered down their podgy noses at the beggars who'd come merely to ask for enough to get through the night had irritated Rosaleen. Fortunately, she'd made sure they'd never again so much as cast a sideways glance at anyone impoverished enough to beg for food. All of them tangled up, mounted, and ready to feed the worms. She wasn't sure how she'd done it. But she didn't regret it.

Rosaleen clapped the soil from her hands, scattering clumps of it in every direction. The late summer breeze was refreshing on her warm, damp neck. Resting her hands on her thighs, she stood. Then she ran her sweaty fingers over the velvet ribbon at her neck, lifting the dark green agate from its sticky resting place in the hollow of her throat. The alabaster rose carved into it shone proudly, even when caked in the day's grime.

The sound of a vanquished threat caught her attention. A young man in dark, tattered clothes and a short-brimmed cap stood with two young ladies and a dark-haired child on the other side of the wrought iron gate. He was shouting, animated. "You 'eard me, go!" he yelled, and she heard footsteps running down the path in the other direction.

Rosaleen turned back to the royal garden, resplendent in red-purple foxgloves and hollyhocks, plump courgettes, and feather-leafed fennel. Back in Ireland, the excess produce alone would've fed her village for two months. Here it was in danger of going to waste, if she didn't hand it out to people like the ones that boy in the patched pants had just run off.

"All for a family who fails to appreciate my efforts," she breathed aloud. "Best be careful they don't find out that I'm secretly doing what they should've been doing all along, tending to those who lack their resources. Those greedy buggers have no concern for anyone but themselves."

She thought about working another hour to make the most of the late daylight. The hydrangeas were being temperamental, and the phlox had begun to wilt. But the appeal of a comforting lavender bath beckoned. So, she headed toward the spacious shed, half-timbered and weathered appropriately for a royal estate. She found it quaint that the king and his family referred to it as a shed. At least an acre in size, it could shelter an almshouse's worth of children with plenty of room to run and play.

In fact, it rivaled the great hall in her village. She'd had fond memories of that place as a child, just down the block from her parents' shop. Sometimes her father would walk her down there on a foggy autumn morning, her hand tucked safely in his, and they'd warm themselves on the hearth of the massive stone fireplace. Their hands and noses thawed, they'd continue to the market for flour and buttermilk. Wrapped in her woolen coat, she'd listen to her father's tales of fishing on the river or milking the cows on his grandparents' farm. They'd bustle back to their rowhouse, modestly but tastefully appointed with secondhand tapestries, silk drapes, and needlepoint pillows on the couch Rosaleen wasn't allowed to sit on. Her mother would bake soda bread, filling their home with the scent of unconditional love and comfort that comes from hard-working hands and is meant to be shared.

But as the monarchy continued to raise taxes, her parents, and everyone else in their village, fell behind on their financial obligations. Furnishings, including the uncomfortable couch, were sold. Then clothes. Then tools. Rosaleen toiled in the back garden to keep herself busy on the afternoons that Mama cried. They struggled to keep their shop open, with so few able to afford to part with discretionary income. And without income from the shop, there was no way to pay the note on the house.

To make matters worse, Rosaleen's mother contracted scarlet fever. Papa had taken extra work at the mill to keep the cupboard from going bare, but he barely earned enough to feed one of them, much less a family. When Mama required more care, they had no choice but to move into the almshouse. There, Mama's fever grew worse. Rosaleen sat with her, huddled in a small cot, and read the Bible aloud, wondering if her mother could hear anything being said. Mama was covered in red blotches and her neck was swollen. She kept her eyes closed most of the time, only opening them occasionally, unable to focus.

Papa had gone to the mill one day when Rosaleen read from the Book of Matthew, the parable of the weeds, in which a man sowed good seed in his field, but while everyone was sleeping, his enemy came and sowed weeds among the wheat. When he returned that afternoon, he, too, had broken out in a bright red rash. He laid down next to his wife, comforting her as she took her final breaths.

"Rosaleen," he'd said to her, "I have earned enough to send you to England. I want you to go there and make a new life."

"But I want to stay with you, Papa," she implored. "You're sick and I want to take care of you."

"No, child. It's too late," he explained, scratching the skin on his throat. "I will be a burden. You will go and find work there. Leave tomorrow and don't look back."

"But I don't want to be away from you," she pleaded.

He took the cameo from around his wife's neck and presented it to Rosaleen. "Here," he said. "I gave this to your mother many years ago. The gift of a young suitor. Take this and we will always be with you."

And so she left, sailing for England and finding work in a boarding house. In her spare time, she'd trim the hedges into whimsical topiaries and plant flowering shrubs in window boxes up and down the block. One day, a nobleman, the earl of someplace she'd never heard of, passed by in his carriage and made his driver stop so that he could admire her work. Before long, an invitation to work at the palace was forthcoming. And ever since then, Rosaleen had tried, and failed, to keep the royal family content with her horticultural expertise.

"Ungrateful bastards," she said, running her thumb over the rose cameo. Parched and weary, she continued to the shed, passing a trio of rose bushes. Newly arisen, their vines entangled the planter boxes which held clumps of ruby-shouldered radishes and tall sheaths of rocket.

"Why, I thought I just trimmed you back the other day," she said, stooping down and enchanted by their heavenly scent. "Now you've got two sisters, have you? And how did you get all the way over—"

She swung her head around and saw that the small rose bush by the Tudor Rose display was still intact. In fact, it appeared to have grown larger. What she saw at her feet was new growth.

"Peculiar," she whispered. She narrowed her green eyes and followed the vines, which trailed to the shed. Then she looked around. Small rose bushes had cropped up all over the garden. None of which she'd planted.

OH, this will surely mean even more work tomorrow after I've already done so much today.

And there was no doubt the king and his family would express their dislike for these straggling roses, popping up willy-nilly in every such place. At least she'd found a way to keep some of them from complaining too loudly.

The half-timbered door to the garden shed swung open with a creak, echoing Rosaleen's achy knees and back. Her eyes fixed on a half-empty bag of soil, delivered by her mysterious benefactor. She still didn't know what that man had wanted, but she was grateful that someone seemed to appreciate the effort she'd been making. And as far as she could tell, the soil was making a difference. Everything seemed to be growing taller and wider since she'd begun using it.

A groan from the back of the shed turned her head. Grimy cheeks shining with sweat as she made her way to the far corner.

Timothy, the king's teenage nephew and a particularly vocal critic of her work, stood against the back wall, resembling a scarecrow. A few days ago, he'd complained that the damsons weren't ripe yet and proceeded to snap branches as he jumped up to pick the still-green fruit. Furious with the royal family for their ungratefulness, Rosaleen seethed.

And then, as her fury boiled into a rage, something strange happened. The thorny vines of the little rose bushes lurched back and forth, weaving their way to Timothy. He was seated on his ample bottom beneath a tree and surrounded by broken branches and fallen damsons. The vines wrapped themselves around Timothy's wrists, shackling him. As he protested, Rosaleen sat back and watched, her eyes cold and flat. Finally, she dragged him into the shed and fastened him to the back wall.

"Maybe you'll learn some manners, like the earl, the marchioness, and all those little brats," she'd said as she calmly walked out of the shed and locked it behind her.

That was days ago. No one seemed to care about the earl, the marchioness, or any of the children. They weren't as popular as Sir Timothy. But now people were beginning to ask where the young viscount had gone. One of his spontaneous hunting trips, likely. Or a dalliance with some courtesan. But no one was sure.

"Rosaleen," he whined, "why won't you untie me? My uncle, the king, is going to have you punished severely."

"So why would I untie you if that's going to happen?" she said, examining the dirt beneath her nails. A good scrubbing was definitely in order.

"You'll rue the day you crossed me," he said, his round face reddening. "You people never understand the privilege of working for the royal family."

Rosaleen glanced up at him, not moving from her position in the dark shed. A smile slowly crossed her lips. "Privilege? You'd know about that, wouldn't you?"

She turned, her heavy boots skidding on the floor.

"Rosaleen! You will not get away with—"

But she smiled and snapped her fingers, signaling for the vines to do her bidding. They scratched his face as they coiled around his neck, tighter and tighter until he was gasping for breath. She snapped her fingers again, before he lost consciousness, knowing he'd not give her any more trouble.

"Goodnight," she said, pulling the door closed as the scent of lavender wafted in the air. Turning her key in the lock, she mused, "That bath is going to feel awfully good tonight."

{ 8 }

CHAPTER EIGHT

Goldie yawned as they crossed the park, headed back to the carriage. Snowy was keeping a tight grip on Goldie's hand. But she didn't mind. Goldie was still a little scared after the young men approached her and Snowy over by the garden gate. She was glad that Freddie had scared them off, but she wondered if they might come back. Goldie's eyes darted around as they crossed the thick, green grass. Better to stay alert.

But she couldn't hold back another yawn, this one louder and longer than the last.

"Goldie," Minty said, "you seem tired. Do you want to ride inside the carriage on the way back to the Observatory and take a nap?"

"Yes, please," she said, drained from the long ride earlier, all the fancy furnishings and gadgets at the Observatory, and then all the excitement of the big city. It had been quite a day already.

Snowy unhitched the horses. "You want to drive?" she asked Minty, who was helping Goldie onto the footboard so she could climb in the back.

"Sure," Minty said. She took a blanket and pillow from the seat and tucked Goldie in. Then she hoisted herself up to the driver's seat and they took off.

As they pulled away from the park, Goldie saw an enormous building in the distance.

"What's that?" she asked, barely keeping her eyes open.

"That's St. James Palace," Snowy said. "See the flag? The one with all the blue, red, and yellow symbols? That's means the king is in residence there."

"The newspaper we read said he's staying at St. James Palace while Windsor Castle is being renovated," Minty added.

"It's so big!" Goldie said. "Can we go take a look?"

"We need to get back to the Observatory," Snowy said. "We don't want to keep Mr. Flamsteed waiting for dinner."

Goldie pouted. "Please?"

"I'll tell you what," Minty said, pulling the reins to steer the ponies in a different direction. "I can take us by the edge, but we can't go up to the palace. You'll have to get a good look from the carriage."

"Besides," Snowy said, "you already saw part of the palace."

"I did?" Goldie asked, confused.

"Yes, the gardens we looked at are the royal gardens."

"But they're so far away!" Goldie said.

"It's a big place!" Minty said with a laugh.

"I hear the king has his own private laboratory there in St. James Palace," Snowy said. "In fact, he's the one who established the Royal Observatory and made Mr. Flamsteed Astronomer Royal."

"They took the old, abandoned Greenwich Castle and refurbished it to serve as the Observatory," Minty said.

"Is that why it's so fancy?" Goldie asked. "With all those pretty tapestries and all of that stuff?"

"Probably," Snowy said.

They pulled closer to St. James Palace and Goldie's eyes widened. It had tall, narrow octagonal turrets framing the arched entrance. Neatly stacked dark brown and red bricks stretched four stories skyward. Several small windows stood in orderly rows along the length of the turrets and over the arch. Everything about it was imposing, from its tall towers to its dark façade.

"Wow," Goldie said, her mouth falling open at the sheer size of the building. "Someone must've spent a lot of time making that."

"It was commissioned by Henry VIII," Snowy said. "It began as a hospital, and then the royal family took it over."

"Why couldn't they just leave it as a hospital?" Goldie asked.

"I'm not sure," Snowy said.

Minty steered the ponies farther off the path so Goldie could get a closer look. She noticed a pair of guards turn and look toward the carriage. One stepped down from his position and started walking toward the carriage.

"Uh," Minty said, snapping the reins, "I think we should go."

"Good idea," Snowy said as the carriage rumbled down the path.

The guard yelled something, then stopped and watched them for a moment before turning around and going back to his post.

Goldie noticed the palace getting smaller as they pulled away. Even though it was summer, the breeze was beginning to cool. She tucked the blanket around her shoulders and leaned back onto the pillow, closing her eyes. Soon, she was fast asleep, lulled by the rhythm of the traveling carriage.

"Is this what you wanted, your majesty?" a lady in waiting asked, offering the queen her ermine-lined cape.

Goldie threw the dark purple garment over her shoulders, banishing the evening chill. "Yes, this will do nicely, Lady Agnes," she said from her perch in the ruby-encrusted chair. Then she stepped off her thrown and tromped about the palace. Its walls were lined with colorful tapestries, depicting famous battles and heralding her ascent to the Crown. Beneath Goldie's small feet, a similar Oriental rug sprawled out, decorated with lions and harps, and entwined with leafy rose vines. She glided across the room, her cape held by a pair of young pages, barely a few years younger than Goldie herself. When she got to the palace's enormous window, she stopped and gazed at the garden.

"Lady Agnes," she called, and the noblewoman rushed to her side.

"Yes, your majesty," came the breathless reply.

"I should like to walk about the garden," Goldie said.

"Yes, of course, your majesty. But I want to remind you that we are expecting Queen Charlotte of Denmark for a reception in an hour. It would be wise not to tarry."

"I want to see the roses," Goldie said.

"Yes, your majesty."

With that, Goldie was escorted to the garden and she stopped and admired the many roses that festooned the gates and brightened the walls. In the center of the garden was an elaborate fountain, spilling over in eight tiers, but it was void of any liquid.

"The water," Goldie said, her ermine cape wrapped around her shoulders, "what's happened to it?"

Lady Agnes mustered a smile. "Water is in short supply," she explained, obviously trying not to upset the queen. "We have decided to conserve what we can so that the people of the kingdom can have access to fresh water."

Goldie shifted her eyes between the fountain and her lady in waiting. "If it's for the good of the people, I will allow it," she announced.

They strolled through the garden, leisurely enjoying the pleasant fragrances and brightly colored flora. Goldie realized Lady Agnes was trying to hurry her along, but she blissfully ignored her suggestions. When she heard Queen Charlotte's carriage pull up to the gatehouse, however, Goldie decided it was time to go back inside.

In her chambers, Goldie stepped into an evening gown made of sumptuous brocade, fitted tightly at the bodice and the skirt looped up in the back. Lady Agnes arranged the gown over Goldie's petticoats and helped her slide into a pair of metallic slippers adorned with narrow silk braids. Once her shoes were on, Lady Agnes arranged Goldie's hair into a crown of ringlets and placed a pair of pearl drop-style earrings on her lobes, setting off her youthful face.

Goldie admired herself in her dressing table mirror for a moment. The palace sure was a long way from the orphanage. But it was her wish to stay here forever.

***

Snowy could hear Goldie snoring and softly muttering as Minty steered the carriage away from the park and headed back toward the Royal Observatory.

"Sounds like she's dreaming," Snowy said.

"She's had a big day," Minty replied.

Snowy looked at Minty. "So did you."

Minty swung her head around as they began the ascent toward the Observatory. "What do you mean?"

"Well, you made a new friend," Snowy said with a smile.

"Oh, Freddie?"

"Who else, silly?" Snowy teased.

Minty tried to hide a secret smile as they meandered over the cobblestones.

"He seems nice," Snowy said. "And I certainly appreciate that he ran off those pickpockets. I guess I haven't been in a big city in a while. Oceans, and forests, and tropical islands, sure. But it's been so long since we've been in London. I think I was so distracted by Goldie and those beautiful gardens that I didn't have my wits about me."

"Don't be so hard on yourself," Minty said, clucking her tongue to coax the ponies up the slope. They approached the bridge that crossed the Thames. Several wild rose bushes greeted them, winding along the path. "It's easy to get distracted with all that going on. But, it was very kind of him to look out for us."

"So, what's his story?"

Minty steered the ponies over the bridge and the carriage jostled from side to side. "Oh, um, he's a chimbley."

"A what now?"

Minty laughed. "A chimney sweep," she said as if she'd ever heard that word before this very morning.

"Oh," Snowy nodded. "That explains the soot on his face and the dirty nails."

Minty shrugged. "Right. He said he works with his father, keeping the family business running. He has some siblings who are too young to work. Their mother is ill."

"Oh, I'm sorry to hear that," Snowy said, genuinely concerned.

"Me too," Minty added. "And then, he said something kind of odd, I thought, this morning. He said that his father often leaves at night to do some kind of business."

Snowy's blue eyes widened beneath the lenses of her glasses. "Who sweeps chimneys at night?"

"That's what I was thinking," Minty said, "although I didn't ask about it. None of my business, really."

"No, I suppose not, nor mine," Snowy said. "Weird, though."

"Very weird," Minty said as they took the road to the Observatory.

"Did he tell you anything else?" Snowy said. The sun was beginning to set and the path was bathed in golden light. She loved this time of day. It was so pretty, and besides, it meant it would be time for stargazing soon. As they passed more rose bushes, Snowy was beginning to wonder why they'd seen so many on this trip.

Minty's words jerked Snowy from her thoughts. "Just that the poor people of London are really suffering. I don't think Freddie's very keen on the monarchy."

Goldie let out a big sigh from the back of the carriage, then started snoring again.

"Mr. Flamsteed said they've fallen out of favor," Snowy offered. "Somewhat surprising since the monarchy was just restored recently, with King Charles II regaining the throne after his father's death while in exile. I guess it didn't take long for the citizens to grow tired of him, too."

"I think it has more to do with the idea of the monarchy in general," Minty said. "I get the feeling that they don't come off as sympathetic to the average person. You know, people are struggling, working more than one job to feed their families. Children are going hungry, resorting to crime. I mean, those pickpockets, they couldn't have been more than a few years younger than us, right?"

Snowy nodded thoughtfully, recalling the scrappy boys Freddie had run off.

Minty continued, "And Freddie said that they have a problem with the water supply in the poorer communities. People are getting sick and they don't know why."

"When Goldie and I were walking, and you were behind us with Freddie, I overheard some people talking about that," Snowy said. "And remember, we read about it in the newspaper on the way here."

Minty steered the carriage onto the cobblestone road leading to the grounds of the Observatory. "I guess all I'm saying is, what good is it to have a king if he can't keep his subjects healthy and safe?"

Snowy paused as the carriage navigated the bumpy cobblestones. "I never thought about it like that, but now that you've said it, that makes sense." She looked at Minty, who seemed a bit fired up in a way Snowy hadn't seen before. "So, what do you think Carter will think of all this?"

"Carter?" the inflection of her voice raised as if she'd taken offense.

"You two have gotten close. That's no secret," Snowy said. "Well, not anymore."

Minty glanced over at Snowy in silent protest to that last remark.

"I know this is all new," Snowy explained. "I'm just wondering where Freddie fits in to all of this. I thought you wanted to be with Carter."

Minty jerked the reins to bring the carriage to an abrupt stop as they pulled up to the Observatory. Snowy fell forward and heard a thud from the back of the carriage.

"Hey!" Goldie said, apparently jostled awake.

"Are you all right?" Snowy said, hopping down from the carriage and throwing open the door to check on the little girl.

"I think so," Goldie said as Snowy pulled her off the floor and set her down. "We stopped so fast that I fell off the seat. I had all these dreams about the palace. And I got to wear a cape with fancy fur and—"

Snowy looked back at the driver's seat, but Minty was already on the ground, brushing off the servant Mr. Flamsteed had sent out to help her down.

"—and then I got to meet the queen of Denmark and—"

"That's great, Goldie," Snowy said, holding her hand. "We're going to go inside now and get dressed for dinner."

They walked into the Observatory's foyer as Mr. Flamsteed's staff ushered them in.

"Dinner will be served in thirty minutes," a maid said.

"Thank you," Snowy replied. She looked around, then turned to go up the stairs. Minty was already at the top, disappearing from her view.

CHAPTER NINE

Minty picked at her plate, barely touching the roasted pheasant or gratin potatoes, which Mr. Flamsteed proudly announced had been grown in the Royal Observatory's garden. He, Snowy, and Goldie were engaged in conversation, discussing constellations, physics, and measuring tools. But Minty was somewhere else. Specifically, in the driver's seat of the carriage, feeling Snowy's remarks about Carter and Freddie sting anew.

She did want to be with Carter. At least she thought she did. But Freddie was so different and charming, and … there was just something about him that drew Minty to him. She couldn't explain it.

"Wouldn't you agree, Minty?" Mr. Flamsteed asked.

Her stomach clenched as a servant cleared her still-full dinner plate.

"What?" she asked, completely unaware of the conversation that had been going on around her. She looked up and saw everyone's head turned, eyes focused on her.

Flamsteed offered a gracious smile. "I said the late summer weather is perfect for stargazing."

"Oh, yes," Minty said, catching his eye. "I would definitely agree."

"Well, then, I propose that we take a look through the telescopes this evening," he said. "It's already dark and I think we'll have peak viewing time in about an hour."

Another servant set a bowl of fresh strawberries and clotted cream in front of Minty.

"That would be great," Snowy said, digging into her dessert.

"I can't wait!" Goldie exclaimed.

But Minty's only reflex was a weak smile, her head clouded with more thoughts than there were stars in the sky. She sat through the rest of the meal, aimlessly digging through the bowl and scooping up strawberries, although she couldn't remember tasting them.

The dishes cleared, Flamsteed stood to usher them all into the telescope room, but Minty shook her head.

"Don't you want to look at the stars with us?" Goldie pleaded.

"Not tonight, little one," Minty said. "I'm tired."

With that, she retired to her room and fell asleep.

In the morning, the sonata of nightingales and mistle thrush gently greeted her. With wide-eyed wonder, she rose and pulled back the heavy velvet drapes, allowing the sun's rays to fill the room. The golden glow of the morning warmed her with its quiet solitude. Refreshed, she quickly dressed and snuck down the stairs, being careful not to disturb anyone.

"Going out so early?" a voice asked from the kitchen.

Minty recognized the woman as one of Flamsteed's staff. She'd been working in the kitchen, her apron dotted with flour.

"I thought I'd get a closer look at that sunrise and some fresh air," Minty replied.

"Sure," the woman said, motioning for her to follow. "You can go out this back door, which will take you to the garden. It's lovely out there on mornings like this."

"Thank you," Minty said as she stepped through the door and into the buttery morning light. Her boots were nearly silent on the ground, the soil soft beneath them. A pair of grey doves fluttered out of the silver birch tree near the doorstep. She watched them travel together, marveling at the way their wings flapped in unison. They landed in sync on the branch of a hawthorn tree at the far end of the garden. One immediately began to preen the other, its feathers ruffling.

She followed them, drawn to their bonded pairing. As she did, she passed boxwood topiaries in large urns and fragrant sweet peas ambling up a trellis before coming to the vegetable patch. The doves cooed, drawing her closer. She stepped past burgeoning radishes and carrots, working her way to the hawthorn tree. A sudden thud jarred her.

Minty turned to the edge of the garden to see a heavy gate swinging open. Then she saw the strapping back of a young man, dressed in tattered, sooty clothes. He backed into the garden, lugging a large burlap sack in each hand. Halfway in, he stopped and lifted the back of his hand to his brow, wiping away perspiration. Then he grasped the overstuffed sacks again and continued to haul them inside.

"Freddie?" Minty asked, causing the man to turn.

"Ah, good mornin', Miss Minty," he said, removing his cap and bowing.

"What are you doing here?" Minty said, hurrying her pace to meet him. "Do you clean the chimneys here at the Royal Observatory?"

"The chimneys?" he said, his mouth stretching into a wide grin. "Ah, no, no. This address is a bit above our regular clientele. But me da' asked me to 'elp out with some of his deliveries."

"Deliveries?" Minty asked, eyeing the two large burlap sacks. "What are you delivering?"

"Uh, not sure, really," he said. "Sometimes me da' takes a little extra work. Doesn't talk much about it. I saw this address on the schedule and offered to 'elp. Thought maybe I might 'ave the pleasure of running into you, again."

Minty laughed.

"Well, not really running into … you know what I mean," he said.

"I knew what you meant," Minty assured. "And I'm glad you came by. This is a nice surprise."

He smiled and Minty heard the doves cooing louder now as the sun warmed her auburn hair.

"So, you're just out takin' a walk then?"

"Oh," Minty said, feeling fluttery inside, "it was such a beautiful morning. I woke up early and didn't want to stay inside. The light was too pretty."

He stared at her lips and leaned closer. "The light. Right."

Minty's knees began to shake, her eyes widening. The doves bolted out of the tree, breaking the silence. Hearing them overhead made her think of Ivan and Evea but they flew off before she could get a good look. "So, uh, tell me about your father," she said.

"Not much to tell," Freddie replied. "We're not particularly close."

She thought back to their first meeting in Stratford and how gruff his father seemed. "Why's that?"

Freddie shrugged. "Don't know, just the way it is, I s'ppose. Never been able to really please 'im."

"That must be difficult," she said. "I'm sorry."

He shook his head. "Don't be. Me da' isn't around much, what with workin' the chimneys all day and then going out at night."

"Does he do that a lot?"

Freddie nodded. "Most ev'ry night. Says 'e goes to these meetings, 'for our future,' as he describes 'em."

"What does that mean?"

"I've no idea, Miss Minty," he said. "There's a big lot of 'em that meet and do some sort of business. I've 'eard talk of drinking and some kind of rituals. 'Do what thou wilt,' according to 'im."

"That's ... interesting."

Freddie shrugged again. "I stay out of it, mind me business, you know? And it's just as well, because all we do is argue when 'e's around anyway."

"I see. And you have younger siblings you look after?"

"Right. But that won't be my problem for long."

"Oh?"

"One day, I'll be the one leaving, startin' a life of me own, you know?" Freddie's smile stretched ear to ear, charming Minty. Then he grabbed the two sacks, gripping each one tightly in his hands. "Well, much as I'd love to stay and 'ave a chat, I've got to finish this delivery so I won't be late to the next one."

"Where's that?" Minty asked.

"The palace," he replied. "Now, can you direct me to the gardening shed? I was told to put these in there."

"Oh, I'm not really sure," Minty said, looking around the property before focusing on a set of small outbuildings. "Maybe this way?"

They headed off, Freddie dragging the heavy sacks. As they crossed the soggy soil path, Minty tripped on something below her boot.

"Oh!" she cried, losing her balance. But Freddie caught her in his arms, dropping the sacks on the ground.

"Careful now," Freddie said. "I've got you."

Minty looked into his friendly brown eyes, bewitched by them. "Thank you," she said, smoothing her dress. Her ankle had begun to throb in her boot, and she reached down to rub it.

"You al'right?" Freddie asked.

"I think so," she said as the throb subsided. "I don't know what I tripped on."

"There's your culprit," Freddie said, holding up a vine. "These roses are ev'rywhere. Bit of a nuisance, if you ask me."

They continued walking, Minty trying her best not to limp as they reached the gardening shed. It was locked.

"Well," Freddie said as he hefted the sacks, leaning them against the wall, "I've no time to wait. This will 'ave to do, I'm afraid."

Minty noticed a small amount of soil spilling out of one of the sacks.

"Now, Miss Minty," Freddie said, cupping her chin in his large hand and tilting it toward him, "promise me you'll be careful and watch out for wayward rose vines?"

She giggled, enjoying the feel of his hand on her face. "I promise," she said.

He was holding her chin in his hand when she heard Goldie call her name.

"Minty! Where are you?"

"Oh," Minty said. "I should go."

"It's al'right. I best be on me way as well," Freddie said, moving his hand to hers and lifting it to his lips and giving it a kiss. "Nice to see you again, Miss Minty. Until we meet again."

CHAPTER TEN

Rosaleen looked up when she heard the thump at the gate.

"Mornin', ma'am," said the young man in the tattered pants. "Delivery for ya."

She peered through the wrought iron bars, eyeing him with suspicion. "You're not my regular delivery person."

"I'm 'elping out today," he said. "Apologies, ma'am. Bit behind schedule."

She unlocked the gate and waved him into the garden.

"Where ya want these?" he asked, lugging two large sacks in each hand.

"I'll take care of them," she said.

"Oh, no, ma'am, they're awf'lly 'eavy," he said. "I don't mind carrying 'em. Ya got a shed or somethin'? Ah, blimey, 'course there's a shed. This is the royal palace, innit? Ya must think I'm some sort of eejit. But it's no trouble, ma'am. I assure you. I can just take these—"

"No. Thank you," Rosaleen said crisply. "I'll take care of them."

The young man straightened his frame, a surprised expression on his sooty face. "Al'right then," he said. "Ya want I just drop 'em, right 'ere?"

"That will be fine," Rosaleen said, masquerading her irritation through a phony smile.

"It's really no trouble—"

"Thank you. You can go now," she said, her green eyes flaring as she pointed to the gate.

He removed his cap, revealing a shock of thick, black hair. "Ma'am," he said, bowing before turning and walking out.

Rosaleen locked the gate and watched until he was out of sight. Then she turned to the sacks and knelt beside them.

"My precious soil," she said, running her hand over the rough burlap. "Like a bit of the ol' sod. I don't know where you're coming from, or who sent you, but you've certainly helped things take root."

She lugged the heavy sacks to the shed, leaning each one against the wall until she could retrieve all of them. When she was done, she put her key in the lock on the door. A muffled chorus of moans greeted her as she turned the key. Swinging the door open, the morning sun sliced through the shed's dark interior.

"Rosaleen," came a husky voice from the back of the shed as she dragged the soil sacks into the shed. "Rosaleen, please."

She ignored Timothy's pleas, busying herself with the arrangement of the sacks. Then she walked over to inspect her tools, looking for the right size shears to work on the boxwood hedges.

"Rosaleen," he pleaded, pulling at his thorny restraints, "I'm thirsty."

She shot him a stern glance. "That doesn't sound like my problem," she said.

"Please, Rosaleen," he begged. "I don't know what you did to the earl and the marchioness, or why you've tied me up but—"

"Because you're a selfish, ungrateful brat," she announced, looking over the collection of shears as she weighed her options. "Your entire family lives in obscene wealth while their subjects starve and fall ill."

"Rosaleen," he rasped, "please, please bring me some water."

She selected a large, sharp pair of clippers, then walked to the back of the shed. The clippers pointed at his throat, she unfastened her flask and dislodged the cap. Then she held it near his face. "Drink," she commanded as she upended it.

He opened his mouth and lapped at the short stream of water, just out of reach. But as soon as it touched his tongue, she yanked it away.

"That's enough," she said, fastening the cap again and tucking it back into her belt loop.

He swallowed hard and gasped. "Rosal—"

"Enough," Rosaleen said. "In fact, I've changed my mind."

"Oh, then you'll let me go?" Timothy pleaded.

Rosaleen threw her head back, her dark hair bouncing as she laughed. "Oh, you'll be going all right." She lifted her hands and the rose vines curled tighter around Timothy's hands and feet, then finally cinched around his neck. His face turned red, then purple, and then pale as life left him. "You'll be going away. Forever," she mused as she swished out of the shed, locking it behind her.

She spent the next hour working on the boxwood, shaping it to her liking. She'd been working on this labyrinth for months, and it was finally growing tall enough to take shape. With the midday sun beating on her shoulders, she stood back to admire her work. Then she walked over to the patch of wild roses.

"Hello, my pretties," she said, leaning down. They stretched toward her, making it easier to snip off a few pregnant buds and tuck them into her trouser pocket with the vines still attached. Then she picked up a watering can and gave the rose bush a generous sprinkling of water. This caused them to perk up, their petals opening wide. "Fancy a drink, do you?"

"Rosaleen!" came an angry female voice from behind her.

The roses recoiled and their vines began to flare.

Rosaleen spun around to see Countess Isabella, the king's elderly aunt, shuffling through the garden. At her age, she didn't get out much. Just as well since she had difficulty with her hearing and seemed to blur the lines of reality and memory. In fact, Rosaleen had once heard her have an entire conversation with her late husband, arguing about the correct proportion of marmalade to toast on her breakfast plate. No matter that her husband had been killed in a tragic hunting accident twenty-six years prior. The royal family seemed to prefer keeping her hidden, and Rosaleen understood why.

"My lady," Rosaleen said with a curtsy. "What a lovely surprise to see you out and about."

"Rosaleen, the lilies of the valley are gone," the countess said in great distress, her jiggly arms flapping as she gestured.

"Yes, your ladyship," Rosaleen replied. "The king insisted that I remove them and plant the larkspur instead."

"No, no, no!" the countess hissed. "They must be torn out immediately. My husband, Lord Albert, detests larkspur. Imagine how he will react when he arrives home from his hunting trip only to discover this grievous affront."

Rosaleen stared at the old woman, the final remaining shred of her empathy presenting itself for consideration. She wondered if her own mother, had she been afforded the opportunity to live to old age, would've wound up in a similar state. The countess' face was deeply creased and her posture was stooped; the years, and the anguish of losing her husband, had taken their toll.

"Well, don't just stand there, Rosaleen," the countess snapped. "Rip out these dreadful larkspur at once and restore the lilies of the valley!"

Rosaleen's empathy dissolved into rage and the rose vines shot forward, wrapping themselves around the countess' wrists and ankles.

"What?" the widow gasped. "What's happening?"

"Countess, I believe you'd benefit from a trip to the shed," Rosaleen said, a wicked grin spreading across her freckled face. "Perhaps you'd like to join Sir Timothy and the others."

"Timothy? And do you mean the earl and the marchioness? All those young children?" the countess screeched. "What have you done with them?"

Rosaleen smiled as the vines did her bidding, then took the countess to the shed. A short time later, her grim task completed, she was back at work, tending the vegetable patch when she heard the king's carriage rolling down the cobblestones.

"Rosaleen," the driver called to her, "have you seen her ladyship?"

Hiding her inner smile, she looked up from a basket of freshly pulled leeks and shook her head. "No," she lied. "I've been working in the garden all day. Why?"

"Seems she's gone missing," the driver said. "It's quite concerning, given that so many members of the royal family can't be accounted for as of late. I'm taking the king and his family to look for her. The servants have all formed another search party, going the other direction. We'll take the rest of the day, perhaps longer, if she doesn't turn up somewhere."

Rosaleen waved as they drove off, and an idea settled into her mind. This was a most fortunate opportunity. She glanced toward the shed. No one would go near it, locked up tight and immune to prying eyes. Besides, except for the king, she had the only key. She looked down at the roses. They were in beautiful bloom now, flourishing, and as pink as Rosaleen's sun-kissed cheeks. With the carriage out of sight, she strode up to the palace and slipped inside.

Everything was eerily quiet. Since the royal family and all the servants were off looking for the countess, the palace was steeped in silence.

She removed her mud-caked boots so she could feel the fine Persian rugs beneath her weary feet. Rosaleen ran her weathered fingers over the silk tablecloths and elaborate tapestries lining the walls, then helped herself to a sampling of berries and tea sandwiches that had been left on the grand table in the dining hall. As she worked her way through the palace's rooms, each more ornate than the last, she found herself in the queen's chambers. Rosaleen went to the wardrobe and sifted through an assortment of bustled ballgowns and skirts.

"How does anyone get any work done in that?" she wondered aloud, running her dirt-coated fingers over the thick velvet bodice of a gown. She removed it from the hanger and slipped it on over her work shirt and trousers, leaving the corset untethered in the back.

Noting its generous size, she mused, "Clearly, the queen has never worked a day in her life."

Then she flounced to the throne room and spied her desired destination, perched on a platform at the room's most elevated point. Rosaleen walked straight to the throne. After ascending the steps, she arranged the voluminous skirt of the ballgown and plopped herself down. Then she hoisted up the gown's skirt and rummaged through her trouser pocket for her cuttings. As she pulled them out, a clump of soil fell into her lap and she pricked her thumb on the vines. A single drop of blood, no more, fell from the deep, jagged slit on her thumb and onto the soil. When it did, the vines became animated, weaving themselves into a circle.

Rosaleen felt a darkness in her chest, where her soul had once been. She sunk into the throne, gripping the armrests and stretching her legs, which dangled above the lavishly carpeted floor. "The royal family can't tell me what to do anymore," she announced, her words echoing throughout the empty throne room. "It's time they learned their lesson. Each of them—in fact, *every citizen of Britain*—will learn the value of hard work, to support their queen. For I, Rosaleen, will soon rule all of England, Scotland, and Ireland."

In her lap, the vines had finished their weaving. She looked at her thumb, barely scratched. In fact, Rosaleen noticed that she didn't feel anything at all.

"And when I'm in charge," she continued, the cameo bobbing at her neck as her voice began to rise, "I'll turn the entire blasted royal family into fertilizer, since they're so full of ... well, at least they'll finally be good for something."

The faraway sound of shouts and chants broke the quiet, but Rosaleen snapped her fingers and listened as the shouts turned to cries. With a satisfied grin, she placed the twisted crown of roses atop her black hair and laughed maniacally.

{ 11 }

CHAPTER ELEVEN

Minty gazed out the window of her room as the sun began to dip below the horizon. Her eyes drifted to the Observatory's garden, and, naturally, her thoughts turned to her encounter with Freddie as the sun had risen that morning.

She wondered what he might be doing now. Would he be on his way home, covered in soot after a long day of making deliveries and sweeping chimneys? She imagined him coming through the door of a humble apartment, his younger siblings mobbing him with hugs while his sickly mother looked on with appreciation. He'd remove his cap, revealing that unruly dark hair, and hang it on a peg next to his coat. Then he'd take off his work boots, piling them neatly by the door.

Minty pictured him flashing that wide, beguiling smile as he moved through the tiny space, stepping over toys and kissing his mother on the cheek. Then he'd go to the basin and scrub the grime from his hands, being careful to get everything under his fingernails. With the clatter of dinner plates in the background, he'd splash a little water on his face, washing away the sooty residue of the day's work.

She was picturing herself offering him a towel when a voice came from her doorway.

"Minty? Minty?"

She spun around to see Snowy and Mr. Flamsteed.

"Didn't you hear me?" Snowy asked.

"I guess not," Minty said, shaking the image of Freddie from her mind. "Sorry."

"I was just asking if you wanted to look at the stars with us in a little while," Snowy said. "It'll be dark soon."

"Oh," Minty said, trying to disguise her surprise. "I, uh, maybe later."

"That's what you said last night," Snowy frowned.

Minty shrugged. "We'll see," she said. "I thought I might just read a book tonight."

"Miss Minty," Mr. Flamsteed said, "I want you to feel comfortable here, as if you were staying in your own home. I'll send one of my staff around shortly to see if you need anything. But please, feel free to join us in the Octagon Room if you're so inclined. It should be a good night for viewing Venus, and perhaps a meteor shower."

Minty raised her brows, feigning interest. "Sounds interesting," she said. "Thank you."

"Well," Snowy said, "we're going to prepare the telescopes. Hopefully we'll see you later."

Minty nodded as they disappeared, knowing full well she had no intention of joining them.

As the sun faded on the garden, she tried to think of Freddie, but her thoughts were as scattered as the rose petals swirling in the evening breeze. She fell back on the bed, her auburn hair spreading around her head like a halo, sighed and closed her eyes. For a girl who was usually rather skilled at thinking on her feet—sailing a ship into mysterious waters and leading her crew in battle—she sure was having trouble making sense of things. It was at times like this that she missed her mother the most. She'd always been the calm voice of reason and a wealth of common sense and wisdom when Minty needed her. Though Minty had soldiered on, growing up without her had taken its toll, to the point that Minty had begun to question her own decisions.

"Miss Minty?" said a voice alongside a light knock at the door.

She sat up on the bed and turned to see a maid in the doorway.

"I beg your pardon," said the short, older woman with the white hair and wrinkled face. "I'm Winifred. Mr. Flamsteed asked me to come by and see if there was anything you needed."

"Oh," Minty said, "please come in."

Slowly, Winifred walked into the room. "Can I get you anything?"

"I'm not sure," Minty said, her eyes glancing toward the window once more, catching the last glow of the sun's rays. "Would you mind just sitting with me for a while, Winifred?"

"I suppose I could do that," the maid said, taking a seat in the chair near the bed. "That's a lovely sunset, isn't it?"

"Mmhmm," Minty mused. "I love the way the sun's shadows fall over the city. Do you live in London, Winifred?"

"I do," she said. "At Glasshouse Yard. Used to live near Rosemary Lane, but we moved closer to the Observatory when Mr. Flamsteed offered me this job last year."

"Rosemary Lane, that's by the docks, isn't it?" Minty asked.

"It is," Winifred said. "Lot of crime in the area. One reason why we were so grateful for Mr. Flamsteed's generous offer of employment."

Minty smiled. "He's a very kind man, isn't he?"

"He is indeed," Winifred replied.

"I've heard a lot about Rosemary Lane," Minty offered. "Isn't there an orphanage in that area?"

Winifred sighed and wrung her hands in her lap, "Oh, there is, and it's such a shame what's been happening there."

"Something about the water, is that right?"

"Yes," Winifred said, fidgeting. "Seems the water there is contaminated, and the children keep getting sick. Poor lambs, they don't have anyone in the world and our leadership ... well ... perhaps I've said too much."

"No, that's fine," Minty assured. "I've heard that people feel the monarchy isn't doing enough to take care of its citizens."

Winifred nodded. "Things are different than they used to be," she said. "If you ask me, no one trusts the monarchy. I mean, what kind of leadership looks the other way and does nothing while children fall ill? Instead, they raise taxes and expect people to work harder. If it wasn't for this job, my family would be on the street like the youths who roam Rosemary Lane."

"Well, thank goodness that's not the case," Minty said, putting her hand on Winifred's. "And thank you for coming and chatting with me."

Winifred stood and lit the candles on the mantle. "Are you sure I can't get you anything?"

"No, I think I'm just going to read for a bit," Minty said, "but thank you."

With that, Winifred left and Minty looked through the bookcases, searching for something to read. But a commotion outside drew her attention back to the window. In the candlelight, she could make out what looked like a group of people, carrying torches and shouting. Though Minty couldn't hear what they were saying, they sounded angry. Fortunately, they were headed away from the Observatory.

"Minty!" cried Goldie, running into the room. "I'm scared!"

Minty swept Goldie into her arms and cradled her. "About what?"

"All those people outside! They sound mean. Are they going to hurt us?"

Minty ran her hand through Goldie's hair. "No, little one, we're safe in here, I promise."

"How do you know for sure?"

Minty sat Goldie down on the bed and pulled the drapes closed. "Well, I have faith that we'll be safe," she said. "Besides, Snowy and I have had many adventures and we've been scared many times. But we always found a way to stay safe."

"Tell me," Goldie said. "How do you stay safe?"

"Oh, let me think," Minty said, cuddling up with Goldie on the bed. "We have lots of wonderful things we've found and used to help protect ourselves, and others. Let's see, oh, for one thing, Noah, I mean, First Mate Carter, has these doves, Ivan and Evea, who never get lost and can always find us. And when we were on our way to rescue you from Mr. von Brock's factory, we found the magic icicle, which can freeze anything solid in an instant."

"I saw you use that when we were running away from him," Goldie remembered. "He was so mean."

"And we used it on Nereus, when we were trapped under the sea," Minty said.

Goldie nodded. "Then he fell overboard and into a volcano."

"He did," Minty said, stroking Goldie's forehead. "And he'll never hurt anyone again."

"Being under the sea for so long was scary," Goldie said.

"It was, but sometimes doing scary things yields great rewards. For example, after we were trapped under the sea, we also came away with the Eye of India, and the Vase of Aquarius, which provides an endless supply of fresh water."

"What else?"

"Well ... oh, I know, a long time ago, we were given the honey diamond, from Queen LuvHoney."

"I remember from our sleepover with Belle, Camille, and Annelise at Snowy's cottage in Epping," Goldie recalled. She rubbed her shoulder. "But I feel like you already told me this."

"Yes, it lets us summon bees, as a token of appreciation from the queen."

"The queen of England?" Goldie asked with a yawn.

"No, silly, Queen LuvHoney," Minty said. "I think you're getting sleepy."

"Can I sleep in here with you?" Goldie asked, curling up on the pillow.

Minty couldn't help but smile at Goldie's sweet face. She was so innocent, and Minty remembered how many nights she was afraid to sleep alone, after her family disappeared.

"Sure," Minty said, laying down beside Goldie until they fell asleep.

***

Snowy pushed back her breakfast plate and sipped the last of her coffee, enjoying the quiet morning. Sir Christopher Wren was due to arrive at the Royal Observatory any minute. The last time she'd seen him was before they left for Bonn. So much had happened since then, and Snowy was eager to tell him about their adventures and hear about his latest endeavors, too. Mr. Flamsteed had mentioned that Sir Wren had been quite busy, working on the renovations to the palace as well as other projects all over London. Surely, there would be many exciting stories to share.

Minty came downstairs, holding Goldie's hand, and Snowy smiled as they sat at the table.

"Good morning," Snowy said, setting down her coffee cup.

"Good morning," Minty said. Snowy was relieved that her friend seemed to be in a better mood than she'd been in the other day.

"Did you get a good night's sleep?"

"Finally," Minty said. "I had a little guest."

Snowy turned to Goldie. "Is that right?"

Goldie nodded as she spread a thick knob of butter on her toast. "I was scared because all those people were so noisy outside," she said.

"Oh, I heard that," Snowy said. "Do you know what that was all about?"

Minty sipped her coffee. "One of the maids said that the people are very dissatisfied with the monarchy," she explained. "I guess they were going to the palace to protest."

Snowy sighed. "Angry mobs going after monarchs," she said. "These are difficult times. I'm glad we're going back to Epping soon."

Minty took a bite of scrambled eggs. "I don't know," she said. "The city's kind of ... *nice*."

Snowy scoffed. "What? You always complain about being away from home in Epping. Why are you suddenly so interested in …" Then she realized what—or more specifically, *who*—was responsible for Minty's newfound penchant for big city life.

She jumped when the knock came at the door.

"Good morning," the voice called from the foyer. Within moments, Mr. Flamsteed and Sir Wren entered the dining room.

"Miss Snowy, Miss Minty," he said, his hand extended as he walked toward them, "how lovely to see the two of you again. It's been so long."

Goldie squirmed and tugged on Minty's skirt as everyone shook hands and greeted each other.

"Sir Wren, this is Goldie," Minty announced. "We rescued her from Mr. von Brock's telescope factory in Bonn."

He squatted down so he could look her in the eye. "Miss Goldie, what a pleasure it is to meet someone so brave," he said as he shook her hand. "These young ladies have told me much about you. I'm so glad you're safe now."

Goldie smiled and hid behind Minty's skirt.

"Well," Mr. Flamsteed said, putting a hand on Sir Wren's shoulder, "what's the good word?"

"Oh," Wren said, standing up, "where to begin? I don't know that good is the word I'd use right now."

They sat down at the table and another round of coffee was served.

"Why do you say that?" Flamsteed asked.

Wren sipped his coffee, "Well, as you know, I've been working all over London on various projects, mostly for the royal family."

"He's been overseeing the renovations on the palace," Flamsteed said, leaning over to Snowy.

"I see," Snowy said. "You really love architecture, don't you?"

Wren set his cup down. "Yes, very much," he said. "But it leaves little time for astronomy, and my other interests. However, before the cold weather sets in, this is the time to focus on building and renovation projects. Besides, who knows how much longer we'll have a palace—and a monarchy, come to think of it—after what I saw last night."

"What does that mean?" Snowy asked.

"I was leaving the palace after finishing my work for the day. And as I left, a very large gathering of people showed up to storm the palace gates," Wren explained. "They're quite angry about the king raising taxes again."

"Dreadful," Flamsteed said. "Were they successful in getting into the palace?"

"Oh, my good lad," Wren exclaimed, "have you not heard?"

Flamsteed shook his head.

"Oh, it's the most extraordinary thing," Wren said. "It seems that as the crowd approached the gates, they were turned away … by roses."

"Roses?" Snowy gasped.

"I assure you," Wren said, "I wouldn't have believed it if I hadn't heard it from one of my contractors who was nearby when it happened. It seems that the roses around the palace gardens have come to life."

"How odd," Flamsteed said, sitting back in his seat.

"That's not the only odd thing," Wren continued. "It also seems that members of the royal family have been steadily disappearing."

"I've not heard of that," Flamsteed said. "How many?"

"Well, I imagine they're trying to keep it quiet, but it seems far more than a coincidence at this point. Now, let's see," Wren said, counting on his fingers. "First there was the earl, the marchioness, and the king's nephew, Timothy."

"That sniveling twerp," Flamsteed muttered. "Probably off with some paramour of questionable breeding."

"One would think that, given his reputation, yes," Wren concurred. "But he's been gone for quite some time and there's no sign of him at any of the royal residences. And then there's the king's aunt, Countess Isabella. No one's seen her in a while, either."

"She's rather advanced in her years," Flamsteed said. "Could it be that they're just not acknowledging the inevitable?"

"Again, one would think that," Wren said, "but there are so many members of the royal court. Some would be about your age," he said, turning to Goldie.

The little girl sat up straight, startled.

"Wait, members of the royal family are disappearing, and no one's talking about this?" Snowy questioned.

"No," Wren said. "But I don't know how much longer that will last. To be honest, I've not seen the king or his immediate family around the palace since they left to look for the countess. And that was yesterday morning."

"How very odd, indeed," Flamsteed said. "What is this country coming to?"

"Not only that, but people are getting sick," Minty offered. "The mob was upset about that, too, weren't they?"

"Oh, yes," Wren agreed. "In fact, I've seen it for myself. I've been working on a building project near Rosemary Lane."

"Where the orphanage is," Minty said as Goldie laid her head against Minty's side. She had a scar there, so she gently repositioned the little girl, smiling down at her.

"Yes, that's right," Wren said, "where all those children have become ill."

"It's so awful," Snowy said. "Do they know what's caused it?"

"Not so far as I know," Wren said. "Something about the water."

"Tell me more about the roses," Snowy asked. "You said they attacked the people trying to get into the palace? How could that happen?"

"I really don't know," Wren said. "But they seem to be popping up everywhere."

Flamsteed stood up. "Come to the garden," he said. "I want to show you something."

They walked out to the garden and Flamsteed led them straight to the rose bush, which had grown at least a foot since the day before.

"This started growing a short time ago," he said. "We've never had roses like this before. It's as if it just came out of nowhere."

"Yes," Wren said, leaning over to take a closer look at the dark pink flowers. "They look like the ones I've seen popping up all over London. Why, there are several of them near the orphanage, in fact."

"But the soil here," Flamsteed explained, "isn't normally conducive to roses. And the *truly* odd thing is that I've not been watering this bush at all. And yet, it's growing like mad."

"Well," Wren said, reaching into the pocket of his coat and pulling out a handkerchief, folded around something. He opened it to reveal several vials. "I took some soil from the palace when I was there. And, I took a sample of the water at Rosemary Lane. These roses seem to grow wild in that neighborhood."

"Can I see those?" Snowy asked, reaching for the vials.

"Of course," Wren said. "In fact, I was hoping we could work on this together."

Thrilled, Snowy accompanied Sir Wren to the Observatory's laboratory. There, they compared the soils and looked under the microscope at the water sample.

"Interesting," Snowy said. "If I'm seeing this correctly, these are gley soils, which are heavy in clay."

"Clay is full of silica," Wren continued. "And inhaling too much silica can do irreversible damage to the lungs."

"Those children who died, they all had a cough and respiratory problems, didn't they?"

"I believe that's right," he said.

"The other thing about gley soils," Snowy said, "is that they can become waterlogged."

"Explains why these roses don't need to be watered very often," Wren said.

"It does," Snowy said. "But the weird thing is that they're similar to what we'd find in Ireland, with all the peat."

Wren stepped back. "Well, that's a very interesting revelation, indeed," he said.

"Why do you say that?"

"The royal gardener," Wren said. "She's from Ireland."

CHAPTER TWELVE

Rosaleen adjusted the barbed rose crown atop her head as she met the carriage. They'd been gone for nearly two full days, and it was late when they returned, but she was determined to take advantage of this opportunity. As the royal family dismounted, she greeted them with a sneer.

"No sign of her ladyship, I'm afraid," huffed the queen, handing Rosaleen a soiled handkerchief. "Do see that this gets laundered. It was a bumpy ride."

Rosaleen glanced at the foul-smelling cotton square, embroidered with the royal coat of arms, then let it fall to the ground.

"Rosaleen," the queen began as the carriage emptied onto the courtyard. "Pick that up."

"I will not," Rosaleen said defiantly, her gap-toothed grin widening. "You don't give me orders anymore. SEIZE THEM!"

She snapped her fingers and at once the rose vines from the courtyard began to coil around the royal family, capturing each of them. They were lifted off the ground and wrapped tight like a caterpillar fashioning a cocoon.

"No, Rosaleen!" the king implored, his feet dangling over the handkerchief on the cobblestones. "Please don't do this!"

"SILENCE!" Rosaleen commanded, and the vines encircled the king's mouth.

The king began to thrash about but quickly saw it was no use. He and his family were Rosaleen's captives. The horses whinnied but Rosaleen told the driver to keep them calm.

"I'll need the carriage," she told him, smiling. "But not for long. Help me get them to the shed and you can take anything you want from the palace."

The king struggled in his restraints, eyes flaring, but the vines tightened around his lips, keeping him quiet.

The driver, half scared and half relieved, helped Rosaleen stuff everyone back into the carriage, drove it to the shed, and helped her string them up inside. Then he helped her into the back of the carriage, where she enjoyed the short ride back to the palace, feeling even more regal in her thorny crown. It wouldn't be much longer.

***

In the morning, Rosaleen made her way to the palace dining room. The angry mob had come close to the palace gates last night, but she wasn't afraid.

Let them break in. Now that I've managed to "weed out" the royal family, I'm sure the commoners will find there's nothing here to loot or pillage. I'm their new queen and this palace and everything in it is mine now. Since the Anglo-Norman Invasion of the 12th Century, England has ruled Ireland. But my ancestors will be vindicated. Druids, pagans, chieftains ... they all resisted the Roman Empire and battled Vikings. The Normans built castles like this for their aristocrats, creating a hierarchy of indentured tenants on land they never had a right to. They even brought their coins, putting us at the financial mercy of the ruling class while building their empire on our hard-working backs.

She helped herself to a handful of grapes, grown from her precious garden, and a thick brioche from the pastry cart as she walked through the dining room. The few remaining royal staff—those who hadn't run off—had learned to leave her alone, lest she unleash her rage. For if they did, unbeknownst to them, she'd have them bound by thorny cuffs and taken to the shed to rot with the rest of them.

Unless she was in the mood to order an execution. That would provide a diversion from the humdrum of the status quo, all these snot-nosed, spoiled ingrates, grousing about their birthright and privilege while never working a day in their lives. She wasn't sad for their demise. Rather, it fueled her.

Rosaleen's wily smile curled across her pale, freckled face as she trudged to the throne room, still wearing her work boots beneath the queen's ballgown and thinking about her journey to England. It wasn't so long ago that a tall, dark-haired sailor had allowed her to board his ship, in exchange for her company. Their time together was brief; he was soon sailing for Maldon and other places and, she heard, working his way up the ranks. But she learned a lot by observing his ruthless intolerance for insubordination, knowing it would serve her well in the future. There was a time to keep your mouth shut and endure unpleasant circumstances, and there was a time to act. Rosaleen had vowed she would never succumb to the monarchy's tyranny the way her parents had. And this young sailor had shaped her view of obedience and vengeance.

She thought of all who had come before her, the sacrifices they'd made as she once again took her throne. Rosaleen sat back, her crown digging into her long black locks, but she felt no pain. Only the sweet satisfaction of delayed gratification. A fulfillment promised in vain but finally realized.

Rumi said that a rose's rarest essence lives in the thorn. For all the pain my ancestors faced from their English conquerors, their unwavering Irish spirit still managed to prosper. We are the architects of field systems, efficiently growing anything in difficult soil and capably feeding our communities until invaders came and ruined it all. Well, the peat didn't fall far from my boots. In fact, it's a symbol of my resilience. The very emblem of my ancestry, proudly marching forward in the face of oppression.

Now, the English will all worship me. As long as they're willing to work.

Shouts from beyond the palace walls jarred Rosaleen from her thoughts. The vines on her head reacted, curling up like armor as she stood. From the window, she could see that another group of people had assembled outside the gates. The crowd was much larger than the previous one, armed with sticks and rocks.

"My people have come," she announced to an empty throne room. The queen's gown dragged on the floor, fraying the hem as she calmly strode back to the dining room.

"Miss Rosaleen—" said a guard, but Rosaleen flashed her green eyes at him. "I mean, your majesty."

Rosaleen nodded in approval.

"What should we do?" he asked. "With so many of the staff departed, I'm afraid we won't be able to defend the palace. We've not enough men left to secure the perimeter. They'll be inside the walls straightaway if we don't act now."

"Let them come," she said, continuing to cross the dining room on her way to the palace's grand foyer. "I am not afraid."

"But Rosa—*your majesty*—this is chaos. This is madness. This is anarchy—"

She spun around, the heel of her dusty boot digging into the lavish marble floor. "This. Is. Justice," she said.

Without another word, she opened the front door, filling the cavernous foyer with the echo of shouts.

"My loyal subjects," she said, arms outstretched as the crowd strained against the gates. The rose bushes lining the courtyard perked up at the sound of her voice, their vines ascending the iron bars separating the crowd from the palace grounds. "The monarchy has had its way for far too long, oppressing the common people while making themselves richer. But they're all gone now, and so, those days are over. As of today, I am your new queen. You will respect my power. And I promise I will reward you, but only if you work hard."

"We can 'ardly work any 'arder than we do now," came a familiar voice from the crowd. But Rosaleen couldn't place it. The young man with the soot-covered face pushed back his tweed cap and raised his arms, invigorating the crowd. "Let us in, your 'ighness."

The mob rattled the gates, shouting angrily in response.

"We don't want another queen, or king," came another voice. "We want to rule ourselves!"

Just then, a large stone hurtled toward Rosaleen, landing inches from her leg. It was followed by another, and another.

Rosaleen gulped, the black velvet ribbon of her rose cameo tightening against her neck as she choked down something she'd not experienced in a long time: fear.

The rose vines lunged at the protestors, seizing and thrashing them about amid a symphony of horrific screams. Simultaneously, the gates crashed to the ground, and the angry mob spilled forward, descending upon the courtyard.

In a fit of panic, Rosaleen ran toward the garden, the place where she felt safest and most comfortable.

"My beauties," she gasped as the mob closed in behind her, "protect me!"

More rose bushes sprung to life, tripping members of the crowd and restraining them in cuffs made of thorns. Stumbling over the hem of the queen's ballgown, Rosaleen faltered but managed to stay on her feet. Then she got an idea.

Hiking up the skirt of the ballgown and reaching into her pants pocket, she produced her clippers. She wielded them in front of her as the mob approached. "It's not me you want," she reasoned, her voice shaking slightly as the rose bushes formed a barrier between her and the angry crowd. "Go to the palace and take it over!"

As the crowd turned back and ran toward the palace, she sprinted to the shed and flung open the door. Timothy, Countess Isabella, the Earl of Gloucestershire, the Marchioness of Nottingham, various juvenile members of the royal family, and even the king and queen had been tethered to the walls with thorny restraints over the last few days. And one by one, the entire royal bloodline had met its fate, save for the king, who was barely clinging to life. As the shouts outside grew louder, Rosaleen took her clippers and cut each of them loose.

"Rosaleen!" the king rasped, weakened by the vines against his throat.

But as he uttered her name in anger, the vines constricted. "What are you doing?" he gurgled. "And why are you wearing my wife's—"

Rosaleen drove her boot into his shoulder as he took his final breath. Then she lifted her clippers into the air, symbolizing victory as the vines of her crown began to bloom. Glossy black roses encircled her head, shimmering like obsidian in the faint light of the shed. "Your reign has ended, your majesty. The king is dead. Long. Live. The Rose Queen."

CHAPTER THIRTEEN

Snowy stepped back and looked at Sir Wren, weighing the possibilities of what he'd just said. "Do you think these roses are coming from ... the *palace*?"

He drew his hand up under his chin, thinking carefully. "Snowy, I'd like to think it's a coincidence," he began. "However, I know a bit about the royal gardener. As you know, I've been working on the renovations at the palace, as well as other projects around London. I'd noticed that the royal gardens there at St. James have grown, so to speak, even more magnificent since this woman took over. I can't recall her name. We've been introduced, briefly. And I asked about her, thinking she might be able to lend her skills to some of my other projects. But the royal family—much to my surprise—wouldn't allow it."

"Because they think she's too valuable?" Snowy asked.

"If they do, they have an odd way of showing it," he replied.

Snowy wrinkled up her nose, perplexed. "What do you mean?"

"The way they treat her, it's as if they don't think very highly of her," he said.

"Then why not let her go?" Snowy asked.

"That's what I find so odd," Wren continued, "because I can see she's quite talented. And I've heard rumors, Hearsay, really. That she may be some kind of, well, *alchemist* might be the most generous way of describing it."

Snowy's nose wrinkled. "Alchemist? Do you mean like a magician? A witch? A sorceress?"

"I don't know about all that. But from what I gather, she came here from Ireland a few years ago, orphaned and penniless. She got the job at the palace because they said she could make anything grow. Everyone says she has an ability like none they've seen before. Astounding, due to her being a commoner, and in fact, Irish by birth. The British have ruled Ireland for centuries, and with much disdain, I might add. And the royal family, well … they're not exactly easy to please. Believe me, in my work with them, I've had to endure many of their …"

"Demands?"

Wren smiled graciously. "Let's say *unreasonable requests,* if you will, but yes. They can be quite demanding. And it never matters to them that these requests aren't structurally sound or that they defy the boundaries of physics. They want what they want. And I know they've treated this poor gardener in the same manner. In fact, not long ago I was strolling in the park, adjacent to the gardens, and I heard the king absolutely demolishing her about delphiniums. Insisting that she rip them all out and plant something else. Delphiniums! So trivial. I honestly don't know how she tolerates it."

Snowy looked out the window to the garden at the far end of the property, letting Wren's words sink in.

"Maybe she doesn't," she offered.

"Why do you say that?"

Snowy pushed her glasses up her nose. "Sir Wren, you said she's from Ireland?"

"That's correct," he said. "Classic black Irish. Dark hair, green eyes. Warm smile. Soft-spoken. Strong work ethic."

"And she was orphaned and penniless, you said?"

"Also correct. Her parents were evicted after not being able to pay their taxes, and then they both fell ill. What are you getting at?"

Snowy ran her fingers over one of the vials. "Have you ever heard that saying, something to the effect of, the rose's beauty is in its blooms, but its strength lies in its roots?"

Wren searched her face. "Interesting. Go on."

Snowy, piecing it all together in her mind, said, "Everywhere we went on our way here, and everywhere we've been, we've seen roses. And everyone says they've just sprouted up, mysteriously, in places they'd never grown before. It sounds like this gardener may have built up some destructive feelings about the royal family."

Wren nodded. "I think I see where you're going, Snowy. There's an Irish proverb I've heard," he said. "The well-fed do not understand the lean."

"Exactly," Snowy said. "Think about the angry mob that gathered at the palace. We know commoners are upset about taxes and children getting sick. They feel like the royal family doesn't care about their subjects. And didn't you say some of the royal family has disappeared?"

"Yes," Wren said.

Snowy couldn't believe the words about to come from her mouth, but she heard herself say them just the same. "So, do you think it's possible that this gardener has decided to get revenge on the monarchy, not just for their abusive treatment toward her, but for the way they've treated their own subjects, and ... the Irish?"

Wren shook his head and let out a long sigh. "Miss Snowy, that's a very dark and troubling interpretation, but to be honest, I'm afraid you may be correct."

Snowy looked at him, still coming to terms with what she'd concluded.

CRASH!

A brick smashed the window at the far end of the laboratory.

Wren ran to the window to look. "Stay back, Miss Snowy," he warned. "Oh, dear, there are even more of them this time."

She looked out the window. A huge, noisy crowd of people was marching toward the palace. Some carried signs that read, "No more taxes," and "Care for our sick."

As Wren picked up the brick, Snowy saw some of the Observatory's staff run outside and check that the gates were locked.

"The roses!" yelled a man passing by. "They've come to life! There's a mob at the palace and the roses are hurting them!"

Snowy's eyes widened as Wren turned to her. But it appeared the threat was over. The crowd pressed on, pumping their fists in the air and shouting as they went. And within minutes, they were gone.

"Are you all right?" Wren asked.

"Psshh, fine," Snowy said. "I've faced greater dangers than that. But, I think I need to get out of here."

"Oh, I don't think they'll be back," Wren assured.

"No, I mean, I think I need to get to the palace," Snowy said.

"Why would you put yourself in harm's way?"

She ran to the laboratory door. When she opened it, Minty was on the other side, her hand poised as if she were about to knock.

"That mob's heading to the palace and the roses are taking over."

"I think I know why," Snowy said.

"I think we need to—" Minty began.

"Way ahead of you," Snowy said. Then she caught Minty's eye and winked. "Glad to have you back on the team."

Minty smiled. "Let's go see what we can do."

They ran back to their rooms and Snowy quickly gathered up whatever supplies she thought they might need. She pulled the chest from her closet and lifted the lid, carefully noting the contents inside.

Honey diamond. Vase of Aquarius. Magic Icicle. Eye of India. Scepter of the Trees.

She had no idea if any of it would be useful. They'd never battled animated roses before.

Minty stepped into the doorway, her rifle slung over her shoulder. "Ready?"

"Almost," Snowy said. "I'm not sure what to bring."

"All of it," Minty said, stepping forward to close the chest's lid. "Tell me about the roses on the way and we'll figure it out when we get there."

They grabbed the chest and hurried to the carriage. Snowy took the reins while one of the Observatory's staff stashed the chest behind the seat. Minty jumped onto the seat beside her.

"Rosaleen!" came a voice from the Observatory.

Snowy looked up to see Sir Wren, standing in the courtyard.

"The gardener," he said. "I finally remembered. Her name is Rosaleen!"

Snowy nodded to him and they tore off, following the noise of the crowd. She explained what she'd discovered with Sir Wren and her hunch about the gardener.

"That's awful," Minty said, "but it makes sense."

"Well, we've got to stop her," Snowy said as they approached the palace. Screams and shouts greeted them as they jumped out of the carriage. The palace's gates had been knocked over and people were running in and out.

Minty pulled the chest from behind the seat and they divided up the items, tucking them into pockets. Just as they were about to take off, Snowy heard a voice behind her.

"What's happening?"

Snowy and Minty swung around, "Goldie!" they said together.

"You can't be here," Minty said. "It's too dangerous, little one."

"I wanted to come with you!" she cried. Snowy noticed that Goldie was wearing a dark green velvet gown, which she recognized from the chest of dress-up clothes the Duke of Somerset had given them.

"Why are you wearing that?" Snowy asked.

"All this talk about palaces and fancy places," Goldie said. "I wanted to play dress-up, so I snuck into your room and borrowed it. Please don't be mad."

Snowy looked at the little girl, then at Minty. A chorus of screams came from the garden. She grabbed the little girl's hand. "Come on," she urged. "We don't have time to lose."

"Stay with me," Minty said sternly. "And do whatever we say."

They ran to the garden and saw the destruction unfolding. The roses had grown much larger from when Snowy had seen them the other day. With sharp thorns and thick vines, they seized people and thrashed them about. To the left, a group of angry rioters formed a circle, kicking and punching whoever was in the middle. And at the far end of the garden, near the shed, a woman with black hair, with what looked like a ballgown over a uniform and a crown of roses on her head, sat on a bench and laughed.

"That's her," Snowy said. "Come on."

Snowy, Minty, and Goldie ran through the mobs, heading toward the bench. But when Rosaleen saw them coming, she took off for the tall boxwood hedges. Snowy followed her into the maze, with Minty and Goldie right behind her.

"Rosaleen," Snowy called. "We want to talk to you."

"You'll never catch me," said Rosaleen from the distance. Snowy tried to follow her voice, but the thick boxwood made it difficult to gain perspective. "I built this maze."

Snowy started to her left, then stopped and looked to her right. Listening carefully, she heard footsteps to the left, so she followed the sound.

"This way," she whispered. But as she turned around to look at Minty and Goldie, they were gone.

***

Minty strained to hear over the noise from the crowd near the garden and beyond its gates. They were banging on the wrought iron bars and chanting now, "Let us in!" As they chanted, the thorny vines curled up the gate, lashing out at the crowd.

"Goldie, grab my hand," she said, reaching behind her as she tried to figure out which way Snowy had gone through the towering boxwood hedges. Once she felt the little girl's hand inside her palm, she turned to her right. "This way."

They walked for several feet, following the shrubbery maze past a series of openings and curved paths on either side, then turned a corner.

"LET US IN!" shouted the crowd. "LET US IN!"

Pots, pans, hammers, and even fire pokers clanged against the wrought iron gates, creating a deafening roar so loud that Minty couldn't hear herself speak. As she got to the end of the row of hedges, she turned, only to find it was a dead end. Frustrated and worried about how long they'd been separated from Snowy, she spun on her heels, nearly jerking Goldie from her feet and causing her to stumble.

"Come on," she said, anger and concern rising in her voice. She hurried back down the row, trying to remember which way she'd come. The sound of the crowd echoed off the metal gates, filling Minty's head. With the boxwood growing so tall, it was impossible to gain perspective. She put both hands to her forehead, trying desperately to focus. She wished she were back on the *G2*, with a handy sextant to help guide her. But that was a luxury she didn't have right now. She looked up at the sun, directly overhead at noon. No help. Desperate for a quick way out of this jam, Minty felt around her pockets for the items they'd brought from the chest. But none of them seemed to be of any use. As a butterfly floated past her face, Minty set her jaw and made a decision.

"This way," she said, deciding to turn back to the right. The noise of the crowd grew louder, causing Minty to think she might be approaching the entrance to the maze, where she could start over again. She passed several openings where the hedges parted. "Almost there, little one," she said, turning back when she got to the end of the row.

But when she did, no one was there. Only the towering boxwood columns that lined the empty path, each of them looking exactly like the others.

"Goldie!" Minty yelled, her heart sinking. Racing back, she looked down each row. All of them were empty. Minty felt her stomach clench as the crowd chanted louder.

"LET US IN!"

She turned around, completely disoriented now. There was no way to know which way she'd come, or which way was forward. She had no idea where to look for Goldie, or Snowy, for that matter. Panic was setting in, but she knew better than to cave to it. She had to stay strong for Goldie, and for the citizens of London who were rallying at the gates.

"Let us in!" said a familiar voice, coming from just behind where she stood. Concentrating on it, she followed the sound as she strode past hedge rows, turning and continuing to the maze's entrance. When she stepped out of the maze, she quickly saw the person whose voice had led her out.

"Freddie!" she screamed, picking him out of the crowd. He was pushed up against the gates, nearly being crushed by the crowd. The rose vines slapped at his face, but he turned away. "Freddie! I need your help!"

She ran toward the gate.

"No! Stay back, Minty!" he yelled, straining against the wrought iron bars. "They'll smash you to bits."

Minty stopped abruptly, realizing he was right as the crowd pulsated against the gates. "I can't find Goldie! She was behind me in the maze and she's disappeared."

The vines suddenly turned toward her. Freddie's eyes widened and he looked up at the top of the gate, adorned with sharp, spiked finials. Minty followed his gaze, understanding what he was thinking and standing defiantly in front of the thorny vines.

"The spikes are too sharp and too close together," she warned. "Besides, the roses will attack you before you make it to the top. Don't do it."

"Where's Snowy?" he yelled.

"Somewhere in the maze," Minty said, hearing panic taking over her voice. "I've lost them both. And the gardener. She's the one who's made the roses come to life and poisoned the water. And we think she's harmed the royal family, too. We have to defeat her before she kills everyone."

"Ah, she's an odd one, that gardener," he said. "I made a delivery 'ere, for me da' the other day an' she was acting like she 'ad some kind of secret."

"A delivery?" Minty asked. "Like at the Observatory? Those big bags?"

"Right, right," Freddie said, bobbing and weaving away from the vines.

Minty squinted, trying to purge the thought from her mind. "Wait, what was in—"

A maniacal laugh rang out from somewhere within the maze, followed by a scream, and she spun around toward the hedges, holding her breath.

"Go!" Freddie yelled. "I'll get in there to 'elp you."

She turned back to him. He was trying to shimmy up the gate, but as soon as he'd get a few feet off the ground, the rose vines would thrash at his hands and feet, and he'd slide back down.

"Freddie! Be careful!"

"Don't mind me," he called. "You go an' find your friends. I 'ave faith in you, Minty."

Faith.

That word calmed her, and she thought of the way Noah had evened her temper when they'd been pulled under the ocean. She took a deep breath and ran back to the entrance of the labyrinth. Urgently trying to recall which way Snowy had turned, she made a left at the first corner. She ran down the hedge row, guided by only her intuition, then turned left again where the path curved. More identical hedge rows greeted her. It seemed impossible to get her bearings.

"Goldie," she cried out. "Goldie, where are you?"

She heard another scream and shot after it, toward the end of the row. As she ran around a corner, she slammed into something and tumbled to the ground. Her head hit the path with a thud.

"Minty!" Snowy said, rolling on top of her. "There you are!"

The girls untangled themselves, nearly tripping over each other again as they stood up.

"Where's Goldie?" Minty asked.

"I thought she was with you!" Snowy said, searching Minty's worried face.

This time, the scream was unmistakable. They both turned to the left and followed the sound of Goldie's screams. At the end of the row, Minty peered around the corner.

"You'll make a fine servant," said the woman wearing the shredded ballgown and gardening boots.

Minty crept closer, but she was horrified as the rest of the scene came into view.

Goldie was suspended in the air, wrapped up in vines and being tossed back and forth.

The gardener laughed again, twirling the vines on her rosy crown.

"You've come to destroy everything my hard work has built," she said.

"No, I haven't!" Goldie yelled.

"LIES!" said the gardener, and the rose vines whipped back and forth, shaking Goldie and making her cry. "My people have made their last sacrifice for England. I will rule over all and then you'll all know what it's like to work for a living. You lying royal brat!"

"I'm not lying!" Goldie said, tears streaming down her face. "Don't say that! I don't know what you're talking about. Let me go!"

Minty looked at Snowy, who'd just rounded the corner, her hand clasped over her mouth. The two of them stood silently, pulling things out of their pockets to show each other, nodding, and calculating a plan. They didn't want to risk saying anything out loud and alerting Rosaleen to their presence.

Minty was sure they'd figured out a way to free Goldie from Rosaleen when she heard a crash of clanging metal followed by angry shouts and a herd of footsteps descending upon the garden.

CHAPTER FOURTEEN

Rosaleen cackled as the dark-haired child cried. Her cherished roses had become quite obedient, reacting to her emotions and attacking anyone Rosaleen perceived as a threat. She had long wanted to cultivate a plant that would act on her behalf and exact her revenge on all who had crossed her. But it wasn't until that soil started showing up that she could make it work. How appropriate that the wild Irish rose had become the perfect vessel for her evil machinations.

The crowd broke through the gates and Rosaleen watched them storm into the palace, leaving her alone in the garden with her captive.

"Let me go!" the child cried again, tears rolling down her green velvet gown.

Rosaleen clenched her hands together and the roses tightened their grip on the child.

"Never," Rosaleen said coolly. "I'm going to enjoy torturing you, little girl."

"My name is Goldie," the child gasped, her face turning red as she was dangled upside down above the reflecting pool.

"Goldie? That's the name they gave you? I suppose it figures. A tribute to wealth, no surprise."

"My real name is Baojin," Goldie explained between clutching breaths. "It means precious gold."

Rosaleen swished her hands from side to side, prompting the roses to toss Goldie in the same direction. She screamed and cried as she tumbled through the air, still restrained by the roses' tight grip.

Rosaleen picked at the grime under her nails.

When will I ever remember to wear my gardening gloves?

The soil was embedded in her skin and mixed with her blood from where she'd pricked her thumbs on the rose vines. She sighed, bored, as the roses continued to squeeze Goldie's wrists and ankles.

"All my life, the aristocracy, the monarchy, they made things more difficult than they needed to be," she said, only looking up to delight in the child's tortured expressions. "They don't care about commoners. They oppress hard-working people, building empires on their backs, and never letting them share in the spoils of success. And what kind of thanks do we get? Higher taxes and fewer services. We've got to work harder and harder just to survive. Meanwhile, the royal family sits on their abundant, padded backsides, pretending they care about their subjects. But your kind doesn't care about us at all."

Goldie was upright now, the color returning to her face. "But I'm not—"

"Shut up!" Rosaleen yelled, adjusting her crown and pushing up the shoulder strap of the queen's ragged ballgown draped over her uniform. As soon as she raised her voice, the roses tightened their grip on Goldie again, making her wince and cry. "I don't want to hear your excuses."

Rosaleen cackled again, delighted that this child was in such distress. She walked closer to the pool, hoping to get a better view of her prisoner's discomfort. "They say there's no rose without its thorn," she continued. "And so, for the sweet, fragrant life you've lived, the life of luxury and beauty, you're going to be punished for the way you've treated commoners. You see, the suffering you and your family have caused left me an orphan."

"I'm an orphan, too," Goldie said.

"Ha!" Rosaleen crowed. "You expect me to believe that lie?"

"It's *not* a lie," Goldie pleaded. "It's the truth. I don't lie."

Rosaleen walked along the edge of the pool, her work boots raising clouds of dust. "Oh, really? Tell me about how hard your life was, Princess Goldie, or whatever your title is."

"It's just Goldie," said the child. "I didn't have parents. I only remember being in orphanages. First, I was in one far away. Then I sailed on a ship and came to another one here in England. In Epping."

"Epping Forest?" Rosaleen asked, suddenly interested in what this little brat had to say. She stopped her pacing and turned to look at the child. "Some of the most enchanting plants grow there."

"Yes," Goldie said, "foxgloves and bluebells."

"Honeysuckle and iris," Rosaleen countered. "And the most exquisite wood anemones."

She let her mind fill with pleasant memories of the flowering plants that grew alongside the towering oaks and silver birch trees she'd explored that summer with her beloved sailor. Their carefree folly of times past warmed her heart. And when it did, the roses began to loosen their grip.

Then she remembered his cruel betrayal, and Rosaleen filled with rage again. The roses reacted, thrashing the child back and forth.

"NO! Please stop!" Goldie cried. "You're hurting my sore shoulder!"

"Orphans are meant to suffer," Rosaleen said, walking along the pool again. "That's why I poisoned the water supply near Rosemary Lane. Those children have no life, and they never will."

"That's a mean thing to do," Goldie said, struggling against the constricting vines. "When the king finds out—"

"Ha!" Rosaleen cackled again and glanced toward the shed behind her. "Not his majesty. I've made it quite difficult for him to say anything."

"But someone will find out," Goldie said. "And you'll go to jail."

Rosaleen walked closer to the pool, swatting away a bee that buzzed by her nose. "No, I'll be busy ruling England," she said, digging her thorny crown into her dark hair. "My wild Irish roses will do my bidding and protect me. But everyone will believe *you* poisoned the water."

"But I *didn't* do that," Goldie declared.

A rumble from the palace turned Rosaleen around. She considered that the mob might work their way to the garden if they found the palace empty. But the thought of torturing this child was too tempting. She clenched her fists, tightening the vines on Goldie's wrists again, and the little girl cried out in anguish.

"I'll tell you what," Rosaleen proposed as the noise from the palace grew louder. "Admit that you poisoned the water, and I'll let you go."

"No," Goldie said defiantly. "I won't lie. I *can't* lie."

Rosaleen waved her hand in the air and a vine slapped Goldie's face. "I will keep hurting you until you admit it."

"No!"

Rosaleen clapped her hands together and the vines walloped Goldie from either side.

"You would do well to follow my orders," she said. "I've already tortured and done away with Viscount Timothy, Countess Isabella, the Earl of Gloucestershire, the Marchioness of Nottingham, even the king and queen. All spoiled, privileged little ingrates."

Another bee floated by Rosaleen, lazily making its way toward the larkspur around the pool. A third buzzed her ear. Exasperated, she swatted it away. Goldie gasped for breath as the roses thrashed her around, mimicking the motion of Rosaleen's hands.

"Admit it, and I'll let you go," she plied once more.

"NO!"

A steady hum was building behind Rosaleen, but she was too filled with rage to turn around and see what it was. Her green eyes flashing, she unleashed a furious roar.

"ADMIT IT!"

***

Snowy winked at Minty as they stood at the exit of the boxwood maze and held the honey diamond aloft. Just as Queen LuvHoney had promised long ago, the bees in the garden had come to the rescue. There were only a few at first, but now a thick, orderly swarm had gathered, and they were heading straight for Rosaleen. Poor Goldie, helpless and frightened in her green velvet gown, was crying inconsolably. As the swarm closed in on Rosaleen, Snowy looked at Minty.

"Ready?" Snowy asked.

Minty pulled on a pair of gloves and then removed the icicle from its case. "Ready," she said. "Distract her and I'll save Goldie."

Snowy looked back toward the reflecting pool. The bees had zeroed in on their target. Rosaleen spun around and shrieked at the black, buzzing cloud about to descend upon her. Screaming, she ran toward the boxwood maze. Snowy stepped back, hiding between two tall hedges as Rosaleen ran past, leaving Goldie suspended in the air.

Meanwhile, Minty charged forward, wielding the icicle. As the rose vines reached toward her, she thrust the icicle against them, freezing them instantly. Covered with frost, they began to snap in various places. Minty tucked the icicle back into its case, slipped it in her pocket, and ran toward the pool, arms outstretched. As the frozen vines broke, they released their grip on Goldie, who fell neatly into Minty's arms.

Snowy watched from her hiding spot in the hedges. As soon as she saw that Goldie was safe, she turned to Rosaleen and the swarm of bees that was following her. They were heading down the hedge rows, with Rosaleen barely staying upright as she dashed down a side path.

"I created this maze," she said, navigating the twists and turns. "You'll never catch me!"

Snowy struggled to keep up. The bees were relentless in their pursuit, surging forward and diving toward Rosaleen. But she managed to elude their sting several times as she disappeared around corners and ran down the labyrinth's intertwined paths.

Snowy came to the center of the maze, where all paths converged. Realizing she'd taken a wrong turn, she closed her eyes. The rioting crowd had disappeared into the palace by now. Snowy concentrated on the sounds she heard. Desperate footsteps, the unmistakable hum of the bees, and the soft coo of doves.

She opened her eyes and looked up. But all she saw was blue sky, which was quickly eclipsed by a thick, dark cloud. She followed the cloud with her eyes and deduced that Rosaleen was only two hedge rows over. Snowy took off running until the sound grew louder.

As she rounded the corner, she saw Rosaleen, tripping and stumbling to stay on her feet as the bees chased her. She followed them through row after row, turn after turn. As they got to the last row, the crown on Rosaleen's head slipped off. Rosaleen, the bees, and Snowy spilled out of the maze.

"Rosaleen!" Snowy called from behind the cloud of bees. "You must surrender."

"Who are you?" Rosaleen asked, backpedaling toward the reflecting pool.

"I don't want to hurt you," Snowy said.

"That doesn't answer my question," Rosaleen snapped. "Besides, my roses will protect—"

A loud shriek came from her lips as she noticed the rose vines were broken and she collapsed on the ground.

"My roots! My strong, hearty roots! What have you done?"

Snowy was speechless as the bees circled around Rosaleen.

"Minty!" a voice called from the area near the shed.

Snowy whipped around to see Freddie, staggering and bleeding. Minty, who had been consoling Goldie on a bench beneath a cluster of apricot trees, stood up.

"Freddie!" Minty called, waving her arm.

The young man started to run toward her, but before he could, a group of people ran by, knocking him to the ground. Two of the men grabbed Freddie and dragged him behind the shed. Minty gasped.

"Stay with Goldie!" Snowy yelled, and Minty hurried back to the bench. From above, Snowy heard more cooing. She looked up and saw two doves circling overhead.

What took you so long?

Snowy returned her focus to Rosaleen, who was clutching the frozen, shattered vines. The bees were in a holding pattern, ready to strike.

"You've destroyed my precious wild Irish roses," Rosaleen wailed. "My babies won't hold up under this kind of frost. They're forever damaged."

"Rosaleen," Snowy said, patiently walking toward her. The bees took their position behind Snowy. "It's not too late to make this right."

Rosaleen stood up and put her hands on her head. "And my crown," she mumbled. "I'm the Rose Queen. I must have my crown."

Snowy kept walking forward, hoping to keep Rosaleen calm as the bees followed. "You don't need that crown," Snowy said. "Not where you're going."

"Nothing matters anymore," Rosaleen said, backing away. "I've lost everything. My parents. My country. My one true love. Everything that was good."

She lifted the skirt of the ballgown and pulled a pair of clippers from her pants pocket.

"And now," Rosaleen warned as she pointed the clippers at Snowy, "I've lost my mind. At least the royal family is no more."

"What does that mean?" Snowy asked, afraid of how Rosaleen might answer.

A long, hearty cackle came from the dark-haired gardener. "Every last one of them has perished, thanks to my precious roses. Tied up in the shed and strangled to death, the lot of them." She laughed again, almost losing her breath. "Soon I'll turn them into fertilizer so that my garden will thrive."

Snowy gasped, hoping it wasn't true.

"And," Rosaleen said, an odd smile on her face, "now you're going to pay for all the pain *you've* caused."

With that, the swarm of bees shot forward, chasing Rosaleen. The gardener ran backwards, but as she got to the reflecting pool, she tripped on the hem of the queen's gown. The bees stung her all over her face, arms, and body. As she tried to right herself, her boot clipped the edge of the pool and she fell in, letting out a final, blood-curdling scream.

Snowy ran through the tall, stately larkspur that lined the pool and peered over the edge. Rosaleen had sunk to the bottom, sprawled out in her gown and work boots. Dead.

Minty and Goldie ran up, but Snowy shook her head.

"You don't want to see this, little one," she said, turning Goldie away.

Minty swallowed hard. "Is she ..."

Snowy nodded. "Yes," she said. "I guess you could say she's been overwatered."

"Minty! Snowy!" came a familiar voice from behind them. "Goldie!"

Snowy turned around and saw Carter.

"Noah!" Minty yelled.

Goldie scrambled out of Minty's arms and ran toward Carter, who swooped her up.

"You look like a princess in that pretty dress," he said as Goldie buried her head in his shoulder.

"I saw Ivan and Evea," Snowy said. "I knew you were nearby."

As everyone embraced, Carter asked, "So, what did I miss?"

Snowy laughed. "Oh, it's a long story. And there will be plenty of time to tell you about it later. How did the repairs go in Maldon?"

Carter gave Minty another squeeze. "Fine," he said. "We sailed the *G2* right down the Thames. But you'll never believe what's happened. Captain Savage, he's escaped."

"What?" Snowy exclaimed. "How?"

Carter slipped his hand around Minty's as they walked. "There was a very powerful earthquake," he explained. We were at sea, testing the *G2*, when it struck. But apparently, when it happened, the door to Savage's cell must have opened, and his chains broke. He walked out, uneventfully, it seems."

"Oh no," Snowy said.

"Does anyone know where he is?" Minty asked.

Carter shook his head. "No," he said, reaching into his coat pocket. "But we did find this."

Snowy looked at the brown, aged leather journal, embossed with a compass. "Let me see that," she said, taking the book from Carter. She leafed through the pages, reading handwritten lines about various topics.

"Well, this is interesting," she said. "Did you know Captain Percival Savage was in love?"

"What?" Minty asked in disbelief. "Who could—"

Carter shook his head. "Being away from someone you love is difficult," he said, shifting Goldie against his shoulder. "I don't judge him."

"After all the terrible things he did?" Minty asked, growing irritated.

"Maybe there's some good in him after all," Snowy offered. "Or at least, there once was."

Carter and Minty stared at each other.

"Pardon me," said a voice at the garden's broken gates. A man with a grimy face and hands, dressed in black. leaned against a broken pillar. "My son, 'ave you seen my son?"

The man shifted his eyes back and forth as if watching for someone.

Snowy shook her head. "No, I don't think we—"

"What's your son's name?" Carter asked.

The man glanced over his shoulder and then hurried off.

Goldie raised her head from Carter's shoulder. "I'm hungry," she announced.

"Let's get you some food," Carter said. "And what are all these scratches on your hands and face?"

Snowy smiled. "I told you," she said. "It's a long story."

CHAPTER FIFTEEN

Goldie was relieved as she, Snowy, Minty, and Carter walked to the carriage. She was grateful to be free of the thorny vines and back on solid ground. Her wrists and ankles were sore, and she had a few deep scratches, but other than that, she felt fine. Her green velvet gown, however, had not fared so well. The hem had been torn and a long rip had split the side. She feared that the Duke of Somerset might be angry with her for ruining the beautiful dress.

As they trudged along, stepping over broken rose vines, Carter talked about the repairs to the *G2*, and said it had gone smoothly.

"I couldn't wait to get here and see, I mean, *show* you," Carter said, smiling at Minty, who blushed.

"It's good to see you, too," Minty said, putting her hand in Carter's.

"Something I'm *not* eager to see is another rose bush," Snowy said with a giggle. "Who knew that something so pretty could be so dangerous?"

As they approached the carriage, Goldie remembered what Rosaleen had said about being an orphan. "Wait!" she exclaimed, stopping at the carriage door. "What about the water? All those children in the orphanage are still getting sick."

Snowy snapped her fingers. "We have just the thing," she said. "Everybody, hop in. We need to get to the river."

"I'll drive," Carter said, taking the reins. Minty sat next to him and Snowy joined Goldie in the back. After a short ride, they pulled up at the Thames, where the *G2* was docked. Through the grayish London mist, Goldie could still make out its tall masts, floating majestically in the breeze. Then she jumped from the carriage and into Carter's arms.

"I've got you, little one," he said.

Snowy rummaged through the chest behind the carriage seat. "Here," she said, pulling out a beautiful, curved vessel. It was a soft aqua blue, with teal green scrolls down the sides that looked like tumbling waves. "When we were trapped undersea with the mermen, they gave us this."

"What is it?" Goldie asked, her eyes widening.

"It's the Vase of Aquarius," Snowy explained. "It provides an endless supply of fresh water."

"I remember how Lyr let us drink from it," Carter said, "just after we'd been captured."

"It was a very thoughtful gift," Snowy recalled with a soft sigh. "A token of appreciation for helping to save the Okeanos."

"Right," Minty said. "And it will be extremely helpful on long voyages, especially if we're unable to find fresh water for a while."

"Can I see?" Goldie asked, eagerly pushing against Snowy so she could get a closer look.

"Careful," Minty said, holding onto Goldie's shoulders to pull her back. "It's fragile."

"The Thames River supplies London with water," Snowy said, gingerly cradling the vase by its handles.

Minty nodded. "So maybe if we pour some of the water into the Thames—"

"It'll cleanse the water, but we'll still be able to use the vase when we sail," Carter finished, smiling at Minty.

"Exactly," Snowy said with a wink. "Now, we just need to find a place to pour it."

Goldie tromped noisily to the end of the dock. She liked the way the wood bounced and swayed below her feet. It made her feel powerful. In fact, ever since being released from the Rose Queen's thorny clutches, she was feeling refreshed and emboldened with a new sense of purpose, though she couldn't quite figure out what it was.

"How about here?" she asked, pointing to an area between the dock and the G2.

Snowy walked up to join her. "I think this is a good spot," she said. "Goldie, would you like to do the honors?"

As Snowy held out the vase, Goldie felt her stomach flip a somersault. "Oh, can I?" she asked, clapping her hands together.

"All you have to do," Snowy instructed, "is hold the handle and pour—"

CRASH!

As pieces of the vase fell into the Thames, there was a massive surge of water. It pushed up all the docks, causing all the ships to rise, and creating a wild, bucking wave.

"Oh no!" Goldie looked down, where jagged aqua and teal shards littered the deck. She started to cry. "It was heavy," she said between sobs. "I didn't think it would be so heavy."

Minty put her arm around Goldie's shoulders. "It's fine, little one," she assured, brushing back Goldie's bangs and pointing to the river. "Look."

Through teary eyes, Goldie saw that as the last drops of water fell from the dock, the river began to gleam. Fresh, clean water had pushed the dirty water outward, rushing just to the edge, then pulling back. There was no flooding, no ground saturation. Only clean water remained. The mist swirled and then dissipated. The water was crystalline for a few moments, rippling with a pearlescent glow as it coursed through the riverbank.

"I think you did it," Snowy said.

"But I broke the special vase," Goldie said, still upset with herself.

"The water!" came a cry from farther down the dock. "It's clean!"

A crowd gathered, murmuring along the bank. A man knelt on the bank and gathered a handful, then took a long sip.

"It's delicious!" he said, eliciting a round of cheers. "As pure as a mountain spring."

Snowy turned to Goldie. "That may not have been the outcome we imagined, but I think the Vase of Aquarius served its purpose," she said.

"But now you won't have it for long voyages," Goldie sighed. "I'm sorry. First I ruined this dress and now I've broken the vase."

"Goldie," Minty said, crouching down, "don't be so hard on yourself. No one's upset with you. The dress only ripped because Rosaleen was hurting you. There's no need to apologize for that. And dropping the vase was an accident."

"I should've made sure you could hold it before I let go," Snowy said. "But it doesn't matter because it ended well just the same."

"Who is responsible for cleansing the water?" came another voice from down the bank.

Goldie stood up straight, shoulders back, chin out. She took a deep breath. "I am," she declared.

The gathering crowd turned and came toward her on the dock.

"Is it you?" asked a boy rushing up to her.

"Are you the one?" said an old woman.

"It's a miracle!" cried a clergyman.

Goldie felt her knees quiver below the torn velvet gown but stood tall. "Yes," she said, "I did it. So that no more children will get sick from the tainted water supply."

Minty, Carter, and Snowy had stepped back, staying within reach but letting Goldie talk to the crowd.

"That's a lie!" cried a man in the back of the crowd. "Someone so young 'asn't got the power to do something like that."

"It's not a lie," Goldie affirmed. "It's the truth."

"Now, 'ow do we know for sure?" asked the man, dressed in dark clothes, with soot across his face. Goldie thought she recognized him but couldn't remember where she'd seen him before.

"It's true," Minty said, stepping forward. "She can't lie."

A loud gasp came from the crowd. Goldie looked around, surveying the faces that were surveying her.

"Anyone can tell a lie," the sooty man said. "Why I bet you've told plenty o' lies, even at your young age, Miss ..."

"Goldie," she said, looking him in his shifty eyes. At last, she remembered. He had come to the gate, asking about his son, before running off. "My name is Goldie."

"Goldie," said the old woman, "the royal family is dead. All of them. We'll be needing someone to rule England."

"Someone like you," said the young boy.

Goldie felt everyone's eyes upon her, unsure of what she should say.

"Well, what do you say?" asked the clergyman.

"I don't know," Goldie said. "I never thought about it."

"England needs a ruler ... who is pure of 'eart," came a familiar voice at the back of the crowd.

Goldie stood on her tiptoes, trying to see his face. But she already knew who'd said it.

Freddie.

"Please," he said, pushing his way to the front and clutching his side, stained with blood.

Goldie heard Minty gasp as he spoke.

"Miss Goldie," he continued, speaking slowly as if in pain, "won't you accept the throne? I know you'll be a champion for the working class. You'll make a good leader, you will. One that will appreciate 'ard work and not impose 'orrible sanctions on those who give so much to their country. Let us lead a comfortable, 'appy life, even if we don't 'ave much to spare."

Goldie watched as Freddie staggered toward her, his dark eyes and wide grin pleading with her. Then he collapsed on the dock.

***

Snowy looked out the dining room window at the palace garden, remembering the chaotic scene that had unfolded the day before. Oliver, the royal family's majordomo, had been kind enough to serve her breakfast between tending to broken windows and other interior damage sustained in the riot. Some of the groundskeepers had quietly dug a grave for Rosaleen and were laying her to rest. She watched as they bowed their heads for a moment, then began dropping shovels full of dirt onto her sparse grave.

May she rest in peace.

"Any word on Freddie?" Minty asked, snapping Snowy from her thoughts.

"Oh," Snowy said, catching her breath as Oliver brought a plate of food for Minty. "Not yet. When we brought him here yesterday, the royal doctor and his team took him back to one of the guest rooms and as far as I know, he's still recovering."

"I hope he'll be all right," Minty said, standing next to Snowy and gazing out the window as the groundskeepers continued their work. "I was worried about him."

Snowy looked over at Minty. "Even with Carter back?"

Minty shot her a glance. "I know, it might not seem like it makes sense. I realize—or at least, I think—I belong with Carter," she said, keeping her voice low, "but I still care about Freddie."

Snowy's brows raised.

"What I mean," Minty explained, "is that I want him to recover. That's all."

Snowy smiled and put her hand on Minty's shoulder. "So do I," she said. "Seems like he risked a lot to try to help us. I'm glad we brought him here for medical attention, rather than taking him to the Observatory last night. Now, how's Goldie?"

"Still sleeping," Minty said. "I think she's worn out from all the excitement."

"The future queen of England needs her rest," Snowy said with a laugh as Minty shook her head. "I'm glad Carter went back to the ship last night to check on the crew and get ready to sail back to Epping later today. I wonder what they'll think when they hear about the citizens of London's plan for Goldie."

"I'm sure Clem will be beside himself," Minty said. "He already treats her like a queen. This will just make it official, assuming she accepts."

"Probably already planning a tea party," Snowy joked.

A growing sound rose behind them and Snowy spun around to look. Carter had sent Ivan and Evea to the Observatory with a message for Mr. Flamsteed and the others, detailing what had happened and letting them know they wouldn't be returning that night. Sir Wren had replied that he'd come by the palace today to see how everyone was doing. But that's not who Snowy saw.

Instead, it was a group of older gentlemen, talking amongst themselves as they made their way into the dining room. Some were dressed in fine clothes, others more ordinary. All wore white. Snowy was astonished to see this large group of men coming toward them.

"Where is she?" asked the ruddy-faced man at the front.

"Who?" Snowy said, shifting her weight a bit and quickly sizing up the crowd. There appeared to be two dozen of them, but from what she could tell, they were unarmed.

"Goldie," the man replied. "We've come to make a request."

"Wait," Minty said, "who are you?"

The ruddy-faced man doffed his white cap and bowed toward them. "I am Sir Francis of Wycombe, a member of the House of Lords. These are my constituents, members of a brotherhood I represent."

"What kind of brotherhood?" Minty pressed, her green eyes narrowing.

"One that is of no concern to young ladies such as yourself," Wycombe retorted brusquely.

"And what do you want with Goldie?" Snowy asked, still not sure if she should trust these men.

"We mean no harm," Wycombe said, his voice and posture softening. "We merely wish to speak with her."

"Here I am," said Goldie.

Snowy turned to see Goldie at the other entrance of the dining room, dressed in a new lavender silk gown and walking toward them.

Wycombe and every man behind him dropped to a knee and bowed their heads.

"Miss Goldie," he said, "we understand that because of you, the Rose Queen is dead, and the water supply in London has been restored. In light of these events, combined with your inability to lie and the fact that every prominent member of the royal family has died or disappeared, the citizens of England have requested that you become our queen."

Snowy observed this surreal scene, unsure of what to say. But Goldie just smiled and listened.

"If you do," Wycombe continued, "we would like to become members of the royal court. My colleagues and I come from all walks of life. Some are members of the aristocracy. Some commoners. But we have all remained loyal to the crown, regardless of the head it has sat upon. At your young age, you will require counsel that only we can provide. We are here today to humbly request that you consider our offer and let us guide you as you make decisions that will affect not just England, but the entire British Empire."

Goldie cocked her head, then looked at Snowy and Minty as if giving the idea careful consideration.

Snowy offered, "Goldie, what do *you* want to do? Do you really want to be queen of England?"

Goldie rocked back on her heels. "YES!"

The men cheered and then took to their knees again.

Just then, Oliver stepped forward. "If you'll beg my pardon," he said, "if we are to have a queen, she will need a crown."

Two men appeared, carrying a jewel-encrusted case. Goldie's eyes lit up and she clapped her hands as the men came toward her.

"We shall work out the details of your official coronation," Oliver announced. "It should be a grand affair, with all of England prepared to greet their new queen. Oh, there's so much to do!"

With that, he whisked Goldie away and Wycombe and his associates left, leaving Snowy and Minty in the dining room.

"Did that just happen?" Minty asked.

"I think so," Snowy said. "Do you think she'll be a good queen?"

Minty nodded. "She's honest and loyal and good-hearted," she said. "I can't think of many more attributes a queen should have."

"The patient," said a voice, "is asking for you, Miss Minty."

Snowy turned to see a member of the medical staff. Minty went with him to check on Freddie. As she left, Snowy turned back to the window, noting that a thick fog had begun to roll in. The groundskeepers had concluded their burial and whatever ceremony they'd held for Rosaleen.

***

Meanwhile, back in Epping, Belle gazed out the window of Snowy's cottage, staring at the withered rose bush at the edge of the property. She thought about the day she came out of the forest, so happy to find Claudette, Annelise, and Camille, who'd taken her in. She was grateful for their kindness but couldn't help wondering what had happened to her family, and how she'd ended up in Epping Forest. If only she could remember.

Belle wrapped a shawl around her shoulders, feeling the first nip of autumn in the air as the fog rolled in. The changing of the seasons was a time for letting things die, like the roses on the waning bush. And for the start of the long wait until spring, when new life would come again.

***

At the palace garden, the dirt was still freshly mounded on Rosaleen's grave. At least her final resting place would be among her beloved plants. Inside the palace, celebratory plans were underway. Squeals of excitement and breathless wonder filled the palatial rooms. But here everything was quiet and still, the air heavy with sorrow and cold, damp fog. As the sun sunk on the horizon, a tall figure emerged from the misty shadows. With heavy boots, he lumbered toward the makeshift grave. A rattling cough came from his chest and his cloak swung with every step until he stopped where the earth was piled up, standing silently. Reverently. At last, he knelt, scooping some of the fresh dirt into his large hand.

"My dear Rosaleen," he whispered as he held the dirt to his lips. He inhaled its scent, then gave it a soft kiss and let it fall from his fingers, onto her grave. "I should not have betrayed you so long ago. So much has happened. But I promise you, my love, we will meet again."

As the sun set, he disappeared into the evening shadows, wrapped in a shroud of mist. And as he did, a single black rose sprang up from Rosaleen's grave.

About the Author

Justin Mitson lives in Garden City, Idaho. A technologist and entrepreneur, he loves to write fun, engaging stories, from children's adventures and mob comedies to deep science fiction and time travel tales. Born in Butte, Montana, he spent most of his childhood roaming around the northwest, living in eighteen different locations before getting through high school. This gave him a sense of adventure and encouraged his imagination. A student of history as well as technology, Mr. Channing loves to ask, "what if?" When he's not writing, he's an avid water ski and snow ski enthusiast (and occasionally does those two activities on the same day) and loves to ride his electronic skateboard on the miles of the Boise area's greenbelt. Above all, his greatest joy is making his wife and two daughters laugh.

www.ingramcontent.com/pod-product-compliance
Lightning Source LLC
LaVergne TN
LVHW012025060526
838201LV00061B/4462